Louisa Cannes is trying to juggle her human resources career with looking after her family and keeping her girlfriend interested. Her ethics are repeatedly tested at the difficult job she depends on to pay for her nephew's life-saving treatment. Cripplingly long hours, an incompetent, lazy line manager and a couple of vindictive rivals don't exactly help, and she is in danger of burning out. But why does the evil boss, Penelope, seem determined to destroy Louisa one minute then groom her for promotion the next? Can Louisa avoid competing with her best friend, can she still call herself a people person, and who can she really trust in the race to the top...?

AN ALEX SPEAR NOVEL

Coming soon from Alex Spear

Out

ALEX SPEAR

PEOPLE

PERSON

Published by:
Shadoe Publishing
Copyright © May 2016 by Alex Spear

ISBN-13: 978-0692712856
ISBN-10: 0692712852

Alex Spear is available for comments at alex.spear@live.co.uk as well as on Facebook @ https://www.facebook.com/alexspearbooks/ or on Twitter @alexspearwriter, on LinkedIn @ Alex Spear if you would like to follow to find out about stories and books releases or check with www. ShadoePublishing.com or http://ShadoePublishing.wordpress.com/.

www.shadoepublishing.com

ShadoePublishing@gmail.com

Shadoe Publishing is a United States of America company

Cover by: K'Anne Meinel @ Shadoe Publishing

PEOPLE PERSON

Chapter One

Monday

There was a time when the thought of destroying another woman's career would have repulsed me.

The idea of causing her to be embarrassed publicly, and for her young children to suddenly have a penniless and frantic mother, would once have been an impossible one.

As I watched Sam writhe, standing there next to the presentation I knew she had spent her entire weekend putting together, I reflected that she and I were the same age. As I watched the terrified smile on her face become frozen and twisted, waiting for the verdict, I considered briefly that she and I probably had things in common. Once upon a time, in my previous life, I would have invited her for coffee or to have lunch together. We could have been friends.

But I was above friendship now.

Friendship makes you weak.

Penelope sat like Caesar, one elegant hand supporting her head as if the polished and informative presentation had been physically painful for her to watch. She turned her trendily tousled head to me and breathed, "What on *earth* was she talking about?" scarcely troubling to keep her voice down. It was apparent to all that Caesar's thumb was down.

I stood and gave Sam a pitying smile. I called across from our table, "uh – thanks, you can go now. That was, well…" and I bitchily let the sentence hang, letting her wait for the magic words "very good" or "not bad" that would never come. Hell, even "average" would have been less damning than the smug silence I treated her to.

I could hardly remember what I used to be like. A friend of mine recently said, with something approaching horror in her voice, "You *have* changed, you know. You used to be so…decent, and thoughtful."

It seemed as if Sam twisted in the wind, like a thing skewered and tormented. After a long ten seconds, she realised I wasn't going to finish my sentence, and she bent her head to gather her things, the tears clearly not far away.

As she fled from the room, I leaned in to Penelope to murmur, "She'll be out by lunchtime."

Penelope gave a long sigh, "Sam always was rather…*reactive*."

It was all I could do not to actually gasp. That word was the kiss of death in Penelope's version of honest labour we had all sold our souls to. It was also palpably untrue of Sam, and I knew that, but made myself un-know it. Penelope's thoughts had a way of taking shape and becoming the harsh landscape I worked in.

I sneaked a look at the tanned, Boden-dressed HR Director.

It would be easy to consider Penelope to be pure evil. Everyone knew it, from the Board who didn't much care what her methods were as long as she achieved the cost savings their pay rises depended on, to the long-suffering staff she picked off seemingly at random.

But then what did that make me? The handmaiden of evil. Mini-me evil. Evil Junior, being groomed for the top.

I went to pick up the last of Sam's papers she had fled without. I did feel the residue of sympathy for her, but quickly squashed it. Her face had been flushed with the pink of humiliation and injustice, tears no doubt obscuring her view. I thought back over the brief three months she had worked at GLC. She had got in Penelope's way, and that had been her mistake. She had been hired as Penelope's 'Project Officer': code for dogsbody. She had apparently worked hard, organised things well and been quite nice. At least, that's what I had heard from my team. I had deafened my ears to this praise, because it was only Penelope's assessment of people that counted for a thing around here.

The trouble started not long after Sam had begun in the role, when she had sensibly pointed out that she was being asked to take on more work than she could get done in her working week, even staying late as she often did. She had let Penelope know this early on so that she wouldn't let anyone down and so that Penelope could either say what the priority was or re-delegate some of the new projects coming in.

Big mistake.

Penelope had taken this, the way she took most communication from her employees, as a threat to her authority. "It's about working smarter," she had purred to an exhausted Sam without giving any clue as to what this might mean, and piling on more work until Sam had done what anyone would have done under the same ridiculous pressure: started to make mistakes and miss deadlines.

Sam had signed her own death warrant. You don't give any impression of weakness, of not being able to cope, in front of Penelope. You blame someone else, you push your work onto colleagues, and you suck up to Penelope and further her career wherever possible. It's your only chance of survival. On hearing that an employee might be human and need to rest and have a balanced life with more than just work in it, Penelope tended to behave like a shark in a swimming pool on smelling a drop of blood.

Sam had admitted to Mike, my immediate boss, in the pub one night that she was attending a weekly counselling session to deal with stress. She hadn't been sleeping and she was looking thin and frail. The next morning she had arrived at work to find herself being 'helped to improve.' Penelope sat her down to discuss an action plan to outline Sam's development needs. What Penelope's version of 'performance management' meant was the most mind-bogglingly petty micro-management, with every tiny decision being endlessly analysed in a negative light.

With every move being scrutinised, Sam had gone to pieces.

But this was Penelope's world of work. In other organisations, so I heard, HR could be a force for good, where the HR Director stood up for humanity and fairness, even when money was tight and there was plenty of hard work to be done. Penelope, on the other hand, seemed to tap the poisonous vein that ran through the profession. The HR she subscribed to was so in love with the sound of its own voice, it had invented the concept that employees could rest by undertaking a different kind of work. And that, rather than pay staff more, a canny organisation could give them higher level duties as a bizarre reward. Penelope referred to such interventions in the hushed tones that let you know she took them very seriously. If you didn't want to get fired, you would be equally humourless in your support of this kind of irrational pronouncement.

Can you imagine being subjected to a humiliating time and motion study that required you to record and explain how long it took you to read and respond to each one of your emails?

That one had been my idea. Penelope had lapped it up.

Did you think the women who work in Personnel, sorry, Human Resources, were fluffy and nice?

I think we used to be. My dad, he's dead now, but he worked in councils all his life, and he was a shop steward for twenty years. Proper, old-school, them-and-us, industrial relations. Back then, according to him, management were aggressive, the unions were militant, and Personnel were the only ones with any semblance of civility. It was Personnel who broke up the fights.

My dad had been devastated when I went into Human Resources. "You'll be a tool of management," he had said, shaking his head.

But he was wrong. Because at GLC, HR *is* the management.

The large HR team, run by Penelope Ross, acted like secret police. We were hated and feared. We saved the company a lot of money and kept the staff petrified. It was a vicious circle. Everyone was bullying and behaving like aggression and political strength were the only currencies, therefore everyone had to behave like that to survive. You had to be tough and insensitive if you didn't want to crumble. We were well paid and if you were prepared to have the ethics of a mafia boss, you could have as much responsibility and "success" as you could handle.

Was it worth it? I went into HR in the first place because I wanted to play fair, and be nice to people who were working hard. I really used to be kind before I got my big break at GLC.

I don't have any excuses. I'm more competitive than I like to admit. I was earning double the salary of most of my former classmates. Facebook was a joy. I had by far the best job title and managed the most staff. My holiday photos were a bit few and far between, but I had so far managed to cling to the status, "Louisa Cannes is in a relationship."

Louisa Cannes, that's me. If anyone can, Louisa Cannes.

I dropped the last of Sam's papers into the bin. No one would be interested in the presentation she had worked so hard on, not now that she was out of favour. Once Sam had gone, she would be universally blamed for all the work she hadn't managed to do. Her reputation would be rubbished, and I would ensure that any references we issued to future employers were damning in a just-this-side-of-legal way.

"Don't forget to update her personal file," Penelope had sighed as she swept out of the room. "Ensure it reflects the steps we took to *help* Sam. Ensure we have records of the *difficulties* she had with her projects."

"Of course I will," I gushed to her retreating back, a picture of professionalism. I would remove any evidence that Sam had got one thing right, from the day she started with us.

Talk about a Cannes-do attitude.

Chapter Two

Back at my desk I breathed deeply. I shoved Sam's file onto my overflowing in-tray and took a moment to study the three framed photos I keep to inspire me. On the left is my girlfriend Liz. On top of my computer is a group shot of me, my mum, and my sister. To the right, behind my mouse mat, is my favourite: the adorable shot of my little nephews: Adam and baby Joseph, taken at their house.

Last night had been the first time in ages I had forgotten all about work, and it was because of my gorgeous nephews. As I had arrived at my sister's house and parked the rust-bucket I inherited from her, I could hear Amanda before I saw her. Screaming at one of her sons. It wouldn't be Eddie as he often didn't get in till nine at night.

She never used to be so stressed. I can remember when she and Eddie were first dating, and she used to come home and tell Mum and me all about it, and I had wanted to be just like my sister; this carefree, laughing, graceful young woman. But now, we were strained with worry for her. Baby Joseph's health woke her in the night, kept her tense and volatile, and finding the money to pay for his treatment meant Eddie had to work himself into the ground.

Staring at the photo of Joseph, his soft chubby cheeks perfect as peaches, his enormous blue eyes gazing in wonder at the camera, I recalled last night. I had hurried to my sister's front door and let myself in with my spare key. "Only me," I called, as I picked my way through the tiny lounge over toys and discarded trainers.

My sister and Eddie had managed to buy one of Swinton's starter homes when Amanda had been pregnant with Adam. It was some special deal to help teachers like Eddie buy a flat, but since the local social housing schemes had been privatised, GLC now stood to gain a lot of extra cash from leaseholders like them. Service charges that kept rising, mysterious improvement works to the outside of the buildings and communal areas, and an exorbitant "general management fee" all creamed off a percentage of Eddie's salary. He had had to move jobs to a sprawling urban secondary school in Gravesend just to get the level of seniority that made it worth them being homeowners, and his long and frequently disrupted journey to work each day meant he saw very little of the kids.

Amanda flew out of the kitchen at me. She threw her arms around me, which was unfortunate as she seemed to have a bowl of green pond water in one hand.

"How brilliant to see you, poppet," she breathed in my ear. "Pureed watercress," she said, presumably to explain the bowl of sludge. "Joe seems to prefer decorating the walls with it to eating it."

She released me, and I handed over the cheque I'd promised towards Joseph's next trip to the specialist in London. "Bless you, my darling," Amanda muttered, awkwardly. She had given up refusing money from me. She knew I would never stop handing it over until Joseph was better.

She raced back into the kitchen and I followed. "Coffee?" she asked, without turning round, but before I could respond we had reached the kitchen just in time to catch Joseph's older brother balancing on tiptoe on a kitchen stool, trying to reach up to something on top of the seven-foot fridge freezer. He tried to jump down before he was caught, but it was too late. His mother grabbed him with a yell. "Dangerous, Adam!" she cried. "Never balance on a stool like that. He's after the biscuit jar," she explained to me. She sat him on her lap. "After dinner," she said to him firmly.

He started to grizzle and Amanda looked despairingly at me. "D'you think you could have a go at feeding Joe for me?" She gave me the pot of bright green watercress puree. "He hasn't had much, and Adam can keep this sobbing up for hours, till his dad gets in."

Adam's grizzling had turned into real howling now.

"No problem."

I took up the plastic baby spoon from Joseph's high chair table top. "Hello, little man." He gazed at me with his enormous baby-blue eyes, and blew a spit-bubble at me. Then he burst into happy giggles and beat his little table top with pudgy hands. I couldn't help but laugh along. He's so chilled. I've heard it's normal for a second child (him and me both), but Joseph is so relaxed and happy all the time. You'd never guess he was seriously ill. I scooped up a spoonful of the organic baby food I knew Amanda would have spent hours preparing for him: simmering, blending, freezing, and worrying about it. I offered him the spoonful. He accepted it happily, chewed for two seconds, then let the bottle-green goo dribble out of his mouth onto his spotless bib. All his clothes were second-hand: charity shop or jumble sale, and boil-washed and repaired till they were fragile and threadbare but perfect for a growing baby who didn't seem to notice that his clothes were ragged and out of fashion. I hoped Amanda hadn't seen him spit out her watercress. She always agonised over keeping him healthy and would be anxious that the nutritious homemade baby food was being spat out.

She was cuddling Adam, who was starting to calm down now. She rocked him and shushed him, his head clasped between her hands, but he showed no sign of letting up the gentle moaning, his thumb in his mouth and a pudgy hand in his mum's hair.

I tried again with a spoonful of watercress, whirling it round Joseph's head first like an aeroplane. He liked this and followed the spoon with his eyes, fascinated. When he ate the spoonful this time, it was with a hearty "um" noise, and soon I could hardly feed him fast enough for his appetite.

"He's had all that, Manda, do you want me to give him something else?"

"No, thanks, I'll have to wash some grapes or scrub some mushrooms for him later."

"You work so hard!"

She flushed. "Not like you."

"Don't be silly – this is the most important job in the world you're doing here."

"Really? Most days it just feels like a depressing battle against two tiny commandos!"

"I'll get the kettle on."

I made us coffee. I knew how guilty Amanda felt about giving Joseph more attention than Adam, and Adam sensed her anxiety and tended to panic. At his age, he understands that his little brother is not very well and has to go to hospital all the time. He's too young to understand that it's a congenital heart defect, and if Mummy and Daddy couldn't find the money for the endless trips to the specialist in London, and for all the extra costs associated with the ongoing operations – travel, nights in hotels, and everything else, then Joseph's future was uncertain to say the least. I stroked Joseph's chubby cheek as I sipped my coffee. His skin had that proverbial baby-smoothness, making an apricot feel like a Brillo pad by comparison. It was impossible to imagine him not being around. And if Eddie and Amanda couldn't find all the money, well then, I would help out for as long as they needed.

I had been so happily lost in that world of family and real caring work that I had floated home last night. I had still been feeling relatively calm until I had arrived at GLC that morning and had to deal with Penelope's scheme to sabotage Sam. Such an unpleasant contrast.

I was still gazing at my inspirational family photos when a voice at my office door made me jump.

In the doorway stood my sweet deputy, Jason. His skinny good looks and self-deprecating sense of humour made him something of the team heart-throb. "Mike's looking for you, boss," he grinned.

I groaned. "Oh, no. Didn't you tell him I'm dead?"

"Guess he wants to discuss your funeral arrangements."

"Thanks, mate."

I looked with weary horror at the emails that had come in while I'd been in my meeting with Penelope and Sam. Sixty-four in two hours? I grabbed my work mobile which had my emails synced onto it. With a stage-shudder for Jason's benefit, I set off for Mike's office.

Mike was my immediate line manager, a conduit between me and Penelope as the Director of HR. He was spineless. I can't think of a better word to describe him. He would flip-flop, U-turn and back-peddle like a circus performer, particularly where Penelope was concerned.

I always took my phone into his office so I could surreptitiously clear some emails while he dithered. Meetings with Mike, or 'catch-ups' as he liked to call them, could take hours, with little focus and achieving nothing except confusion and frustration.

PEOPLE PERSON

Sometimes I would distract him by asking about his favourite topic: internet dating. He was still living with his wife but they hated each other, and she had a new man she would stay with at weekends. If you ask me, Mike didn't want his wife to fully leave him because she still did all his washing and cooking, and kept his house immaculate. She was financially dependent on him and seemed not to have the confidence to break away with her new beau. Mike explained the set-up as him 'being understanding of her needs.' He had told me with pride that he spent his evenings in his home office, eating the dinner his wife had made him, while flirting with other women in chatrooms. He had even shown me his brilliantly fictitious profile picture: a photo shopped image of his eldest son, who is thirty years younger with a five stone less gut.

I suspected Mike had been on the internet searching for a chatroom the IT Department had forgotten to block when I had come in. He moved the mouse a bit quickly and was slightly flustered.

"Ah, Louise!"

He always called me Louise. I'd given up gushing, "hey, you know what?...actually…it's Louisa!" in a proactive yet respectful tone.

"Things OK?" he beamed.

I considered this. "Well, we've got two people off sick all this week: one stress, one exhaustion. That, coupled with your idea to reduce all standard turnarounds by a day, has set us a good challenge."

"Great, great…" he sighed happily, not listening, returning to his computer screen.

He was oblivious to my murderous stare. That slashing of the turnaround times was crippling us. We had to publish a customer charter, setting out how quickly each piece of work we did would take. Fair enough, but the timescales had already been shaved to the quickest we could possibly manage with a full team, and then out of the blue, Mike had announced that we were going to get everything done in a day less. It was typical Mike, an attention-grabbing initiative with no basis in reality. He didn't understand any of the processes my team carried out, and had a cheery ignorance of the time they took to complete.

He thought he managed over fifty staff. In fact he was a lucky blagger, completely dependent on a raft of resentful middle managers like me. He didn't contribute anything. He took the credit, until something went wrong, when he would somehow create the impression that he was in no way connected with that team. Rubbish managers like him were supposedly found out and dealt with since GLC had rebranded itself as a lean and efficient business rather than the clunky local government department that had stood on the same site. It just wasn't true. Mike was living proof that sycophantic passengers could survive anywhere.

"I'm overspent on the budget again this month," I said, trying to get his attention back. "All elements are fine, except the staff travel expenses, which you knew about. How did you get on at that budget-setting meeting?"

The budget for staff travel expenses had clearly been set years ago, and it was about a tenth what it needed to be, with my staff regularly travelling to meet customers and run through the work they paid us to do. At first I had panicked when I realised the budget was being blown, but having reported it up the line to Mike month after month and him being so relaxed about it, I assumed I had done my job. In the end I had suggested he negotiate for the budget to be set at a higher, more realistic amount, and had furnished him with plenty of evidence to show why we needed a bit more money. The only thing I couldn't do for him was meet Penelope and fight our corner. That was part of his role, and goodness knows he did nothing else.

"Ooh, sorry, I meant to say I forgot all about that meeting," he grinned. "I must have been busy with something else and it completely slipped my mind. Soz, Louise, soz."

I groaned inwardly. Mike had missed so many meetings; I wasn't convinced I was getting all the facts I needed. I had to get out and talk to other people to make sure that all the messages Mike should have been cascading down, were getting to me and my team.

A sharp little knock on the door behind me made me virtually snap to attention. Only one member of GLC knocked like that.

"Can I have a word?" Penelope sighed, coming in and sitting down, prompting Mike to flounder with his mouse and frantically close some website or other down before she could see. "Oh, Louisa, I'm glad you're here too. I'm very concerned about your budget, Louisa. *Consistently* overspent, and no evidence of financial control or forecasting. I don't feel confident."

It was all I could do not to squeak. Keeping my voice even, I told her, "uh, Penelope, I have been flagging that the staff expenses are overspent and have been creating regular forecasts." I desperately wanted to say that I had been sending them to Mike, and if he hadn't passed the implications of my forecasts up to her, it was because he hadn't understood them. But I had seen how he treated his managers if he thought they were dobbing him in, and I needed a good reference if I ever managed to get out of here.

"The financial reporting has not got up the line to where it needed to be, Louisa," Penelope scolded, as if I were a wayward child. She addressed me: her sitting, me standing. It was humiliating, and it must have shown in my face that I was considering setting her straight, because Mike shot me a warning look. "As the budget holder, Louisa, you need to be on top of this," Penelope continued. She then turned away, and proceeded to talk to Mike about me as if I weren't there. "Budget monitoring training, I think, and set a review period. We need to help Louisa to improve on this."

Mike nodded sagely. "That's right," he said, doing his best impression of a competent manager. "I wasn't kept in the loop about the overspend, and that's disappointing. I'll be giving Louise some robust feedback on this. But we must make some allowances for her age."

My blood was boiling. How could he sit there and lie like that? But he knew I wouldn't get him into trouble. He went to too many meetings with Penelope without me, and would have ample opportunity to run me down. He knew I needed him, so therefore he knew I would protect him.

The age attack stung, though. I was by far the youngest person I knew who had got to this level of responsibility, working my way up rather than being on any kind of accelerated graduate-training management scheme. I had done it by being organised. I played fair with people and I worked bloody hard.

None of this counted for anything in the next thirty seconds. Feeling a bit like a cornered animal, I could very carefully extract myself or I could find myself savaged and left for dead. My career was thirty seconds from over. Twenty-nine, twenty-eight...

"Penelope, I felt I had managed the situation but apparently not the way you would have liked," I managed to say. I saw Mike visibly relax. He knew he had got away with it.

Penelope continued to observe me with a sarcastic smile. Not half an hour before, I had been doing her dirty work. Did she have no loyalty to anyone?

Perhaps I had nothing to lose, then. If she was going to attack and criticise me, what was the point of helping her further her aims by carrying out unethical orders? Was I any different from poor Sam?

Well, yes, I was, I thought, as I forced myself to give a penitent smile to my two laughably titled "superiors." I still had a job. Whereas Sam, who had stood up to Penelope and pointed out the injustice, was now unemployed.

"Every day is a school day," beamed the impossibly smug Mike. "We all have to learn at some point. Even I did, although when I was your age I didn't have such a nice job as you! I didn't earn so much and I had to work late!"

I worked late every night, and at weekends. He didn't know that because he had no idea what I did. He wouldn't last five minutes doing my job, yet he got paid twice as much.

I needed to get out of Mike's office before I said something regrettable. "If you don't need me, I'll get back to work...?"

Mike gave a sly look at Penelope, who gave a short nod. "Yep," he beamed, "off you go, Louise. Thanks! Good catch-up!" he called. I slunk out of the office, my mind a whirl of resentment towards my hateful manager and the two-faced Director.

I quietly closed the office door, putting as much focus into shutting it gently as it took to keep me from ramming their heads through it.

Chapter Three

So what was this job I was killing myself for?

GLC was a recently privatised social service. It was a company that existed to make a profit but the main aims were to run housing and office space for the Swinton community. Swinton residents are on the whole a conservative bunch, averse to change, but when the show had been run by local council officials, unfortunately the former organisation's reputation had been for wasteful bungling. The council sold off the department and with it, the chance for a business to run the services and charge residents for doing so.

The glossy marketing brochures we now published showed convincing figures to evidence improved services with reduced costs. Who knew whether the promised improvements had really been made? The spin was the important thing, and dynamic young managers like Penelope Ross were masters at it.

Last summer, there had been a vacancy created for a general manager with HR knowledge and I had stayed up late for weeks prepping for the interview. Mike, Penny, and Rupert had seen some potential in me and I had been grateful for it to say the least. Swinton does not have many well-paid jobs. It is a suburban town mostly designed for commuters to get into London. Small but respectable houses line up around a station, two pubs, and a church. There is a choice of two schools: the noisy comprehensive I went to, and a fairly cheap private school in the leafy outskirts, where we border with posher Aylham.

I managed a large team. I had an army of hard-working first- and second-jobbers. Bright and willing school leavers. What they lacked in formal qualifications or plummy accents they made up for in graft. We were given tons of donkey work: lots of support stuff to the rest of the company. Personnel, admin, customer service. The team was large but for the work we needed to get through, it was pretty lean. The thing was, we're mostly young and positive, wanting to be helpful, so in her drive to maximise profits and have ever more impressive results to report to the Board, Penelope would frequently pick on us to make savings and absorb more of the department's work.

Juggling people and posts to balance the ever-dwindling salary budget, I had had to ask members of my team to swap round the work they were doing. They had had to get used to sudden changes to job titles, being extremely flexible in their duties, helping each other out by coming in on the weekend at short notice, things like that. I hated to mess them around so much but usually my team were so sweet, they just got on with it. If there was ever a grumble I would just take them all to the pub that Friday night and leave my personal credit card behind the bar.

Going back into my little Perspex-screened office in the middle of the open-plan Shared Services area, where all my lovely team sat, I shut the door. Mike must have at some point in the past accidentally given me access to his email inbox. I can imagine how he would have done it, the klutz, probably trying to find a way to delegate work and meetings to me. Anyway, because of his mistake, I've found that I can have a peek at what emails have come in to his mailbox. I've never told him this as I don't want him to take away the functionality. Being able to see the emails he is receiving from Penelope that he would rather keep secret from me has come in very useful.

I had a hunch that something was up when Penelope had been asking about budgets. I was fuming but needed to stay cool and get information. Logging in to Mike's emails, I scanned down the subject lines. Lots about Viagra and Russian brides, as usual.

Then I saw it.

Shared Services Restructure.

PEOPLE PERSON

I checked my office door was shut and I diverted my phone. I needed to look at this carefully.

I opened the document. It was even worse than I thought.

Penelope was looking to make cost savings, we all knew that. But her plan was particularly fiendish this time. Rather than the relative dignity of just outsourcing my team's work and making us all redundant, she had decided to actually make us compete for our own jobs against outsiders.

I didn't even dare call her a bitch in my head. So strong was her presence and her all-pervading power, I had fallen in to the department-wide mind-set that she would somehow get to hear of any criticism, even the silent kind.

According to the document, the first wave of the Shared Services Consultation was to begin that Wednesday afternoon. After that, the hell she would put us all through was scarcely comprehensible.

I closed the email account down and stared at the blank screen for a full ten seconds, inwardly calling Mike and Penelope every name I could think of. What was I going to do?

I needed moral support. I grabbed the phone. When it was answered, I blurted out, "hi, I know it's not Friday, but –"

I stopped. I would not cry.

The comforting voice at the other end said, "you sound upset, babe. Give me ten minutes. Meet me in the Thai place."

Sunna and I went for lunch together most Fridays. Generally at GLC, there was no time for any more than a sandwich at our desks (plus my endless comfort-snacking throughout the day) but we treated ourselves once a week to a proper lunch away from work. I needed her to keep me sane. She was the only one I would admit to feeling less than sure of myself to.

She arrived two minutes after I had. In her bright fuchsia pink sun-dress and jewelled sandals, she looked like something out of Vogue. She plonked herself down and let me spill my guts, not interrupting.

"Keep calm, babe," she drawled when I'd finished ranting about my meeting with Mike and Penny, and how he had deliberately got me into trouble to save his own neck. I wasn't sure yet whether the restructure was too confidential even to share with my best friend, particularly in a public place. When you work in HR, it's a fine line between being professional and just needing to confide in someone. She seemed to sense I had more to say, but didn't rush me. "If you panic and jump ship, and take a pay cut, just to get out of this place, then the GLC bastards have won."

I loved Sunna for her casual swearing. She was brilliantly suited to her role as an HR Business Partner. Assertive and proud, she *hated* being told what to do by anyone. She always had to argue and stand up for herself. She would say that a childhood as the youngest of six, growing up in an explosive estate in Brixton, had been the training she had needed for a career in hustling and tough negotiation. Even people who didn't like her had to grudgingly respect her.

She ordered her usual: red Thai curry with jasmine rice and a beer. I was on yet another diet and went for the chicken and papaya salad with a vodka tonic. The crazy hours I work mean months go by and I won't have been to the gym. I have the best of intentions but they go out the window when I'm stressed, and I'd already had a doughnut and a Snickers bar that morning.

As the little guy took our order, I glanced around again to make sure there had been no one from GLC in the café when I had let off steam.

"Relax, we're the only ones that ever come in here," Sunna said, one hand on my arm. "You're getting paranoid. By the way, you're looking exhausted, girl."

"Gee, thanks."

"I'm *serious*. You got dark circles. You need a holiday."

I blew out my breath, "Maybe Liz and I will manage a long weekend after the…sorry, can't say."

"The *what*, honey?" Sunna could always tell when I was properly worried. And I was about this. She leaned in close and put her hand on my arm.

I could trust Sunna. I knew that. "It's a restructure," I whispered.

"Damn," she announced, to the restaurant. We got a few funny looks.

"I know. Just Shared Services, as far as I know. But it looks like we're up against outsiders for our contract."

"*Mike,*" she spat.

"Exactly."

What we didn't need to say to one another was that Mike's days were numbered. He had been promoted way above his level of competence and was proving to be an expensive liability. Shared Services was his empire and certain areas of it had too many staff who could be getting through a lot more work if they had proper direction.

It made my blood boil that he could claim the credit for my efficient little band. And we were vulnerable because we were lumped in with his failing hotchpotch of teams who had long given up trying to be inspired by him, and were now just cynical and obstructive.

"Anyway," I mused, "What I meant was, when all *that* is over, I hope Liz and I can get away somewhere."

Sunna gave me a huge grin, "Look at your eyes light up when you say that girl's name."

I smiled back, no doubt flushing a little. But it was true. Oh, Liz.

Liz was the love of my life. It sounds cheesy, but it's true. I first saw her working in the IT department; this tall, angular young woman in the classic geek uniform: Atari T-shirt and jeans. And I had fallen in love. I had been virtually open-mouthed at this vision of lesbian beauty. I had had to avoid my opening line being, "hello, could we get married and have babies please?" Rather than, "My computer won't work, could you come up and fix it, please?"

The funny thing was, I had never been particularly into that type of girl before. If I'd had a type, I would have said some hunky cliché like that one off the L Word, you know the one I mean. She's a bit skinny for me but the kind of women I normally go for aren't really on TV much. I'd had a few girlfriends, one serious, but then when I met Liz, it had felt as if my love life was just beginning. I couldn't imagine ever not being with her. When we were alone together, talking, I felt as if I could really be myself. I had wondered whether dating a colleague would be awkward, and so we had a pact not to discuss work. That had been her idea. But it had quickly become one I was grateful for, particularly as time had gone on and I had ended up doing more and more things at work I wasn't at all proud of.

Sunna was checking out her favourite waiter. She was perpetually dating, but had never to my knowledge got serious about any guy. She seemed to have more fun window-shopping than making that final purchase. "Ohh, yes," she whispered to me, the mischief clearly in her voice, as the guy bent slightly over an empty table to gather in the glasses.

"You're obsessed!" I whispered back.

"Oh, that reminds me," Sunna said, a huge grin in my direction. "I've got tickets for the Beefcakes this weekend. You in?"

The Beefcake Superstars were like Swinton's version of the Chippendales. They were local boys stripping in the less classy of our two pubs for charity, and a night out with them was supposed to be hilarious. "I can't," I said, taking an angry swig of my vodka. "There's no way I can get away without coming in to work on Saturday and Sunday, and any spare time I've got, I've just got to see Liz. We haven't had a proper date in about four months. Even a night together watching TV would be a start."

"Well, if you change your mind...."

"If I get bored of my fillet steak at home, I'll come out with you for beefcake. We're still on for Body Pump on Sunday morning, though?"

"You bet. I need to be beach perfect if I'm going home this summer. The sands of time do not flow upward," Sunna groused, waving her fork at one of her slender thighs.

"You're kidding. I'd kill for your figure. And where you put all that food, I have no idea." I checked my watch, "Better get back."

"Keep me posted on the *restructure*," Sunna whispered, "And don't work too hard."

"Yes and no," I smiled. Thank God for a friend I could trust at work, and one who really knew what it was like to work for Penelope Ross.

Chapter Four

Tuesday

The restructure seemed to move through quickly. The Board had no doubt been won over by the cost savings it would mean. Even before the main consultation meeting I knew was coming, Penny prepared the ground by picking off a few small fry posts in her endless rounds of reorganisation. Even with my secret heads-up, I wasn't expecting it, which of course was one of her methods to keep us all on the back foot. So it was that the next day, Penelope summoned me to her office to tell me that the receptionists' posts needed to be reduced by half.

As you entered our offices, we had a bank of desks with three of my people who worked as a formidable team. They got through a huge amount, organising the incoming work and allocating it to the rest of their colleagues, and getting rid of time-wasters with charm and humour. They didn't earn a huge salary; it seemed criminal to decimate their numbers, and force at least one of them to leave altogether. But that was what Penelope's new structure demanded.

"You want me to manage with only one and a half on reception?" I had squeaked, then instantly regretted it.

Penelope had the look of death. In the presence of weakness, her eyes became cold and dead.

"Well, if you feel you need your comfort blanket – " she began to hiss, clearly calculating how to destroy me.

"No, no," I hurried to interject. "Just confirming the parameters, Penny. Absolutely fine. Can do."

Given no information about this one from reading Mike's emails, I had had no chance to think through how I would deal with this horrible situation. I had decided to be honest with the three of them. Sian, Melanie and Kimba.

I walked in to the reception and Sian had given me an innocent smile. "Good morning," said Kimba in her cheery Irish accent. Mel turned round in her chair when she heard me come in and looked pleased and expectant. I felt so guilty. They had been in the first year of our secondary school when I had been swanning around in the sixth form, captain of just about every girls' sports team, popular and cocky. They had followed me to GLC as I was something of a role model still. Also, I was their boss, and they trusted me. How could I have led them to such an undignified workplace?

"Can I see you all for a short meeting?" I muttered. Their faces fell when they saw the look on mine. I shouted through to Jason, "Could you organise reception cover for half an hour?"

In they trooped, to the small windowless office we could borrow for meetings. Their little faces broke my heart. Sian looked close to tears already.

"I'm so sorry, guys," I started, "I need to be honest with you here. Your team of three needs to be reduced by one and a half posts. It's a cost saving, and it's not a reflection on any of you – you've been fantastic."

Sian looked shaken. Kimba comforted her, while Melanie remained more composed. "How are you going to choose?" she asked with a formidable maturity for her nineteen years.

I had thought this through. "If there's any way you can choose between you, that would be best," I said. "Did any of you want to go part-time?"

"I could, for a short time," Melanie said slowly, "and maybe then you could keep all of us, maybe things would change?"

"I could do some extra child-minding," Sian sniffed, "That way I wouldn't miss the money from here, quite so much."

PEOPLE PERSON

"If anyone really *has* to go, I could move back in with my mum for a bit," Kimba said. I knew she had just started renting a flat with her boyfriend and it meant the world to her to be there. Their sacrifices were so much to them, and would mean so little to the company.

I saw red then. Goddamnit, Penelope wasn't going to have to give up anything, was she?

"Thanks guys, leave it with me. Take a nice long lunch break before you go back to work, won't you." I stormed off to Mike's office.

Knocking on his door, I counted to five to let him close down his dodgy website, then let myself in. Mike was looking flustered and mock-casual. He sat back in his chair, letting go the mouse once he was sure the screen was non-incriminating. "Louise…"

"Hi Mike. This restructure. Were you involved when it was decided on?"

"The wha – oh, yes, yes, of course. I was involved – my empire, you know." He really believed it. "Penelope could see I was the man for the job."

"So how did you decide which areas to trim down? You must have looked at capacity, I guess? How did you identify that my team had too many staff and your other areas couldn't be trimmed?"

His blank look didn't last long. Mike's gift was in his blagging. "Oh, it was an instinctive move," he grinned. "I observe all my teams closely and I knew your guys could handle it. You're flexible, and tough. You'll bounce back."

"You mean, we're the best, so we have to manage with the fewest resources?" I checked.

"You got it, Tiger."

I decided to be a little devious. "I've got so much to learn from you, Mike," I purred. "Could you talk me through the figures you used?"

"Figures?" The blank look was back, but it was more panicky now.

I knew it. He had no clue how much work my team were getting through every day. He also was far too pally with the accountants who worked in his Treasury team. They made money so they were untouchable. They had a reputation as a rather sexist, obnoxious crowd. I didn't know them well. All I did know was that they included in their number, Rupert, Penelope's stuck-up boyfriend.

There were some funny rumours about Rupert, actually. Something about him being a bit too handy with his fists. Still, in any organisation you get gossip, and I had no idea what the truth of the story was

"Yes, you know, you must have compared the output of the staff in my team with that of, say, your Treasury team, and made a decision that the Treasury staff were already working flat out. Of course, if you'd spotted that, oh, I don't know, for example that your Treasury staff *didn't have enough work to do, and were coasting-*" it was all I could do not to wring his neck, "you would have made savings there and left us alone. Could you share your figures with me? I'd love to learn how you make that kind of important decision."

He kind of looked like a goldfish that had been dragged out of the tank. He was gulping, gasping for air, in a very discreet way he probably wasn't even aware of.

"No – no need to bother yourself with all that, Louise," he stammered. "All done and dusted now, you just keep up the good work, eh?"

"Could you talk to Penelope about my question?" I spat as a parting shot. "I'd love to learn from you both, so I'd really like to see the figures you used to decide to cut my team rather than Treasury. If you don't ask her, Mike, I will." I wore my confident face until I was safely out of his office. Inside, I felt sick with dread, at the damage they were planning to do to real people, just to further their own careers.

Chapter Five

I took my team for drinks that night. I thought we could all do with cheering up. Even if I wasn't crazy about what I had to do for it, I had to admit having a good salary was amazing.

By the time I got to the Old Gate Inn, most of the usual suspects were already there. Sunna was at the bar with our mate Rosie, the Head of Payroll. They both turned and waved at me as I came in the double doors. I shrugged off the stress of the day and gave them both a grin. "Vodka tonic," I mouthed at Sunna. She rolled her eyes and hollered back, "we know!" She was on some kind of enormous cocktail by the looks of it, with complicated straws and fruits exploding out of the glass, which seemed to be filled with layers of pineapple and cream. I didn't know how she could afford the calories.

The Old Gate Inn is the larger of Swinton's two pubs, and the more relaxed. A large wooden-floored dining area had been installed when one of my former classmates had taken over as the live-in publican. Plush sofas and charming mismatched coffee tables gave the snug a pleasant living room feel that lent itself to a chilled after-work pint. In the summer we spilled out into a beer garden with a treehouse for the kids. It was the only option for me, considering the aggression of the other town pub, where a woman wearing more than her underwear was considered to be a lesbian, and "lesbian" was a term of abuse.

I shouldered my way through the five o'clock rush of customers to the large table my team had commandeered. Jason was impressing the girls with the latest jokes from his stand-up comedy routine. He was always rehearsing his material, trying it out before his next pub gig. Kimba and Melanie were at one end of the table, still looking upset following our meeting. Sian was nowhere to be seen, presumably having been too upset to come out, and had perhaps gone straight home. They were with their other friend, Stacey, who used to work on reception with them but had recently been promoted to Treasury Assistant. She worked with the group of accountants managed by Mike and had got herself a decent pay raise. I was pleased to see her again.

My battered stalwarts were my priority, "What you having, Kimba? Mel?"

"Hiya," they turned and said to me. It broke my heart how professional and nice they were, even when they were being pushed around by the company they worked so hard for. "I'm all right," said Kimba, waving her glass which was still half full, and Mel said, "I'm driving, anyway."

"Stacey?"

"Oh…well, thanks very much, another one of these, then, please."

"No problem." She was on some kind of lurid alcopop. "Anyone else?"

I looked round the rest of the table with pride. They behaved more like they were my family than my colleagues. I felt responsible for them.

Suddenly, an unwelcome face appeared at the window. "Is that Carly?" She was Penelope's PA, and she had that syndrome that some assistants and secretaries have, where she thought she was all-powerful, because she had the ear of the boss. In Carly's case it was probably true, because Penelope adored her and the way she did her dirty work for her.

I was surprised to see her enter the pub, wave frantically to my team, all smiles, and plonk herself down in the middle of us all. "Alright, pets?" she trilled.

Carly was short, pretty, curvy, and seemed to dress mostly in white lycra. She seemed to be everyone's friend. Everyone said they loved Carly, and everyone secretly knew you couldn't trust her as far as you could chuck her. Smiling, 'up-for-it' Carly, always ready with banter and sexy charm, always ready to put the boot in to a rival. Carly was as ruthless as a particularly unethical cobra.

"Er, hello?" I forced myself to say to her. I really wasn't in the mood for Carly.

"Thought I'd come down and congratulate you on dealing with Sam last week," Carly breathed with a gleeful glint in her eye. "Sam had been struggling for such a long time, and I was so impressed how you resolved the situation."

Was that just last week? My destruction of Sam seemed to have happened years ago. I felt slightly sick at the memory. I didn't want congratulations for doing a shameful part of my job; I wanted the oblivion of alcohol.

"You did your bit too," I reminded her, nastily. "You took the notes for Penny and recorded Sam's failings, as Penny saw them, anyway."

Carly was giving me a knowing look and I realised she was trying to provoke me into criticising her beloved employer, so she could report back to Penelope my disloyalty and get me into trouble. What a stirrer! I introduced her to a couple of others who were sat near us, to offload her onto them, and when they got talking, I slid out of my seat under the pretext of getting more drinks in.

I went and stood near Jason and his harem of adoring girls. I listened in to the joke he had them rapt with.

"A man goes into a library and says to the girl behind the counter, 'fish and chips, please.'"

Leigh was laughing already, as if the opening sentence were the punchline. She was slightly flustered and seemed not to know what to do with her hands in front of Jason – fiddling with the straw in her drink, then smoothing her skirt so it reached slightly further down her thigh.

"The girl says, 'don't you know this is a library?'"

Jason looked down at his drink, making the audience wait just the right length of time for the denouement. His hair was cut in a long dark curtain which fell over his eyes. He was skinny and tall, all arms and legs, though he never stopped eating.

Abbe glanced at Leigh. Leigh never took her eyes off Jason. She was only just twenty, with a little cherub face like a doll.

"So the man says, 'oh, I am sorry.'" With a final flick of the fringe, Jason looked up and did a stage whisper: "'...*fish and chips, please.*'"

Abbe shrieked with laughter. Leigh seemed too stunned by the sudden eye contact to laugh at first, but recovered and joined in. I had to chuckle. Jason was such an unassuming lad. He had a real gawky charm that made the delivery of his jokes much better than the material.

A sudden hush fell over the table. I was astonished to see Rupert plonk himself down in the seat I had been about to sit in. What the hell was going on? First Carly, now one of my least favourite peers at GLC. These people never wanted to mix with us. They liked The Swan with its cheap drink deals and regular brawls. Something was most definitely up. Rupert was flanked by two colleagues from the Treasury department, all dressed like city lawyers rather than the public sector workers they were.

There's no denying that Rupert was a beautiful man. He looks a bit like Jude Law, but his eyes are more intensely blue. Icy.

"All right, girls?" Rupert breezed, deliberately including Jason in his greeting.

"And boys," Jason muttered, his head down.

"Yeah?" Rupert spat, suddenly moving his face close to Jason's, which became more hidden by the curtain of hair, "Grown a set since last Friday, have you?"

I didn't like the edge in his voice. I recognised this kind of sledging, and my instinct to protect my team-mate was like fire in the pit of my stomach.

"What's this?" I asked.

Jason flicked his hair and I could see his cheeks were somewhat reddened. "Nothing, boss."

"Tell her!" Rupert jeered, egged on by his mates who still stood, one on either side of him, pints in hand.

"Tell me what?"

The sections of Jason's face visible between the dark curtains of hair were so red that they looked almost purple. He said nothing.

"Showed him how men settle an argument," Rupert crowed, "This wuss couldn't hack it, and went crying to hospital."

"Did you two really have a fight?" I asked. I couldn't believe it of Jason. "What on earth about?"

Leigh piped up. "Rupert said something really horrible about me." She looked quite nauseous at the memory of whatever the insult had been, "Jason stood up for me."

PEOPLE PERSON

"This whole thing sounds very unprofessional," I said loudly. What I meant was, Rupert should stop telling HR about his disgusting exploits or I was likely to have to do something about it. A fight with a work colleague in their own time was a grey area, and the less I knew about it, the better.

"I put the wuss in hospital," Rupert continued to brag, seemingly oblivious to my warning. "Broke his jaw, his arm, how many ribs?"

Jason seemed unable to say anything, but one of Rupert's mates gave him a hard shoulder nudge and pushed him visibly in his chair.

"Three," Jason said in almost a whisper.

"Look, now I know about this, I can't just ignore it," I said to Rupert, trying not to let my fury show. "If you've beaten up a colleague, that reflects on you at work. I'll have to look into what happened as an HR matter."

"Just you try it," Rupert spat, standing up and preparing to walk away, followed by his sneering cronies, "Who do you think your boss is?"

Having Penelope as his current girlfriend was a real trump card. Impotent in the face of his arrogance, I went very cold and still. He put his face right in Jason's, and shouted, "Watch your back, wuss! Don't forget."

Jason just sat there, his eyes down, angry and silent, waiting for it to be over. Rupert laughed at him, and me. "That's right. You both may as well work for me." He loped off, and we breathed again.

I would get revenge, I swore it to myself. No matter how long it took, I would take them all down: Penny, Mike, and especially bloody Rupert.

It wasn't until they'd gone that I realised Rupert and his mates had charged their drinks to my credit card behind the bar. As if they didn't earn enough already! That's always the way with rich people – Rupert had come from a loaded family, but is he generous with it? Nope. Always looking for freebies, handouts, things he can claim back through GLC expenses. Whereas Sunna and I haven't come from much, but now we're earning a decent amount, we feel lucky and we share our good fortune with those around us.

What an awful day. I downed another double and felt my head start to spin. The music playing turned to all our favourites, meaning someone had commandeered the jukebox. Putting my arms round Jason and Leigh, we started the customary singalong. *Tragedy! When the feeling's gone, and you can't go on!* we all roared out, complete with synchronised hand-gestures. Then, that Rihanna song about drinking to the freakin' weekend. Singing at the tops of our voices, in our drunken band of friends, started to ease the pain just a little.

Liz came to collect me around seven. As the manager, I tend to leave a night out early so the team can relax. Also, she'd suggested we go for a bit of a date night, before I forgot what she looked like.

I took back my credit card from behind the bar, and gave it to Jason. "Deputise, my friend," I said to him.

He gave me a mock salute. "I live to carry out your instructions, boss. And get the team drunk at your expense."

I was glad to see him back in his chipper mood. Rupert wasn't worth ruining your evening over.

"Do your duty, soldier."

Chapter Six

Liz drove me the short distance to our little flat not far from Swinton high street.

"It's so good to see you," I whispered, ruffling her hair as she drove, "What a horrible day. How was yours?"

"Fantastic," she grinned. Liz loves computers, she could play with them all day and wouldn't want paying. "I managed to get to the bottom of that bug we found last week…" She launched into some explanation of a complicated fault she'd managed to fix.

"I have no idea what you're talking about," I crooned in her ear, "but you sure look sexy when you say it."

I left her on the sofa in our flat, while I ran up to our little bedroom to find something nice to wear for our dinner date. I really wanted something she hadn't seen me in before.

I had bought a sweet floral dress for Joseph's christening in a month's time. It was a bit dressy for the Chinese restaurant Liz always took me to, but she was worth it.

I pulled it gingerly over my head, mindful of the delicate silk.

I could hear my mother's voice in my head, saying, "Careful! It might not be big enough for you!" Something she would often say if I were borrowing my sister's clothes.

I have a photo of the four of us, stuck in the frame of my full length mirror. I stared at it now, noticing how much younger I looked in it next to my glamorous older sister and protective parents.

I had thought, back then, that everything would stay the same forever. It had seemed inevitable that my dad would be the head of the household, keeping us all safe and comfortable with the money he seemed to magic out of the air.

Every family has a myth.

In mine, growing up, my mother's myth was that my sister, Amanda, was perfect, whereas I was trying my best but just wasn't as blessed as my older sibling. My mother's refrain would be, "poor Louisa." The things I didn't really mind about myself, our mother tried to make me feel better about. She almost pitied me, I think, and subjected me to affectionate teasing. Amanda was tall, whereas I'm just a little dumpy: short in the leg and solid in the waist. Amanda has long fair hair, like Mum's, while mine is dark and resolutely curly, more like Dad who was a quarter Greek.

I still couldn't believe my dad was gone. He seemed unstoppable. His Greek family called him The Bull. Mad hair, a great wide head with laughing eyes and a boxer's demeanour. He was never defeated by anything, so how could death have been enough to take him away from us?

I like to think I was my dad's favourite. He loved us both, and doted on Amanda, but he and I had a lot more in common.

Amanda excels at graceful feminine accomplishments like ballet, piano, and being diplomatic. My friends would say that I'm an honest, energetic tomboy who grew into a half-decent leader. I know I often say the very thing I shouldn't, but my friends tell me I'm straightforward, and that there's no side to me whatsoever. If I've got something to say, I say it openly – I just can't see the point of bitching behind someone's back, or bearing a grudge, come to think of it.

Maybe that's why I find the bitchiness at GLC so hard to take. I don't do it myself, and I suppose I can be naïve, as I expect everyone else to be as honest as me. Unlike a lot of my colleagues in the HR department, I am a manager of staff. I head up a team of twenty or more and I am proud of that. Never the brightest or best-behaved at school, I have finally made good, using my (some would say) likeable style of organising people to become, hopefully, a fair manager.

PEOPLE PERSON

Maybe knowing the history of my immediate family helps explain where I am coming from. Amanda and her perfect husband, Eddie, have two gorgeous children I adore. Joseph, the youngest, was born with a heart condition that needs lots of extra money to fund the right care for him. My mum and dad always used to help them out a lot with money, because even with Eddie's reasonable salary as a teacher, giving Joseph all he needs for a really comfortable life costs a heck of a lot of money.

Then out of the blue, my dad died of a heart attack. He was found slumped at his desk, only in his mid-fifties. What none of us had realised was that he had been borrowing from his pension to help out little Joseph. Dad had presumably thought that he could pay it back later by working past retirement. There had been times when Amanda had come back from the consultant's appointment, telling us about the options for treatment that would be so much better for Joseph but not available on the NHS, and Dad had always insisted that his grandson was going to have the best, and said, "we'll raise the money, we'll manage." I didn't question where he had been getting the money from. I don't know whether my mum had known the truth.

Now that Dad was gone, Mum was unexpectedly left without much money at all. Mum's main source of income now was her widow's pension, but it didn't go as far as Dad had hoped when he set it up, because shortly before his death, he'd re-mortgaged the house. My mum would now have to continue to make repayments for the next twenty years. She had been a housewife since Amanda was born and had no skills or confidence to launch herself into a dire job market at the age of fifty-six.

Since my dad passed away, the dynamics of our family had changed forever. Suddenly, the two women I'd spent my life feeling inadequate alongside – gorgeous, graceful, delicate – were looking to me to be strong for them. Unlike the two of them, I'd never assumed a husband would financially support me (always having been much more interested in girls). I'd taken courses and worked my way up in a profession I was reasonably good at, and had always paid my own rent and bills.

I couldn't be more different from Mum and Amanda. When I was growing up, if my mother had glanced idly through Vogue and seen a beautiful handbag she simply had to have, she had only to pout at my father and he'd buy it for her. Dad had been an old-fashioned Essex boy who'd always expected a wife who was essentially a dolly bird on his arm. Mum had spent her adult life more or less as his pampered pet. Amanda, of course, had adopted an identical approach with Eddie, and had never considered working herself, as she was a wife and mother.

If I had wanted a handbag, it always seemed fairest to earn the money and save up for it. Probably my father would have given me the money if I'd ever asked, but I loved the feeling of satisfaction that came from knowing everything I had and enjoyed, I had paid for myself. I got twice the pleasure that way. It also made me feel closer to my father, when he was alive, knowing that both he and I were people who worked.

Maybe that explains a little bit about why I'm so driven by work. Having always been the tag-along, the slightly ugly-duckling kid sister of the family, I was suddenly the bread-winner. I was the girl who'd had the sense to invest in something that would last, while the two beautiful swans found they had been chasing illusions and had very little to call their own. They didn't have to ask me for money – I gave it to them gladly. I loved them. However annoying they can be, you always stick by your family. Earning money for them made me feel very proud.

I could hear Liz padding up the stairs, complaining that she was starving. "Just a sec." The dress fit well, surprisingly. I'm not fat exactly, just solid in a Greek way, but I've got big boobs that usually ruin the shape of a bodice. But this looked good: the button-through front was roomy enough not to be straining round the bust, and the narrow belt nipped in my waist. Cap sleeves and a full skirt completed the picture.

I felt Liz's cool hands round my waist. She had crept up behind me as I had been looking at myself in the full length mirror. "Nice dress."

"Hello, you," I purred.

"Hungry?" she asked, her eyes holding a different question.

I kissed her. "Dinner can wait. Let me show you how these buttons undo."

Suffice to say, the dress didn't stay on long.

Tangled in each other's arms and legs, we lay bathed in our own sweat, getting our breath back. I'm so unfit these days.

Our double bed was definitely too small. It was the one Liz had bought for herself. I had moved in with Liz soon after we met.

PEOPLE PERSON

Commitment-phobic Sunna had been horrified at me giving up my independence, as she saw it, but I had known Liz was right for me and trusted her with my life. I adored living with her, and it meant I did actually get to see her around my crazy working hours.

I stroked Liz's cheek, "Are we going out for dinner, or what?" I teased.

She had her hands protectively on my body. "Yes. Need to keep your strength up," she growled. "You might need some more energy before the night is out."

"Again?" I giggled, mock-girly, "You are insatiable!"

I'd have to pay for dinner again, I was sure.

She clambered out of our bed and started to get re-dressed. Her jeans jingled with change in the pockets. Liz is South African, and when she first came here, no firm would give her a break and without any money to go to the pub and so on, she was isolated without many friends and with no family. She's a sociable type who loves to talk, and she had become very homesick and desperate to talk to people back home. She missed her family and her handful of really close friends from school. She managed to rack up a huge phone bill, the fool, through naivety rather than design. She'd struggled to find work for months, had already gone through her savings, and couldn't pay the bill.

I don't know what made me think of it now. Maybe the way she looked so confident, striding around our bedroom, full of post-coital triumph. It was hard to think of her ever having frailties, but I knew that she had buried the helpless feeling of being in debt she couldn't repay.

Instead of contacting the phone company to explain the situation, Liz had brazened it out, ignored the problem, and hoped it would go away. Stupid, but haven't we all done something like that? Anyway, she kept throwing away the letters that kept arriving without even opening them and the issue snowballed. Cutting off her phone was only the beginning. Liz had innocently thought that would be the end of it. She'd used a service she couldn't afford, and the service had therefore been taken away. How wrong she was. Debt collection agency fees, lawyers, extra costs on top of the original bill, and finally a court summons. Of course she failed to turn up, and was promptly given a CCJ and court costs.

Liz grabbed my hands and pulled me up to a sitting position in our tangle of blankets and pillows. "Shake a leg!" she was grinning at me, "Couldn't you eat a horse, now?"

"Yes, but my legs are still weak, you stud." I groped for my clothes and staggered off the bed.

Thank God Liz had managed to get on the books of a supplier of IT temps, and had money coming in now. She had found work doing IT contracting at GLC and was finally paying back the debt in monthly instalments, although the court order that was recorded against her name proved to be an inconvenient punishment. It made it very difficult for her to get anything official in this country, so it had to be my name on the tenancy and all the bills. She was still working through a dodgy employment agency who didn't carry out any checks and didn't ask too many questions. She could be earning much more if she could go 'legit,' but accepted her lot without question. She was older now and felt embarrassed about the trouble she'd caused in her adopted country. I think she almost enjoyed repaying her huge debt, to feel as if she was contributing to her new home.

"Chinese!" we shouted at each other, and burst into giggles. As long as between us we had enough money to cover our bills and have a bit of fun, I was happy.

Chapter Seven

Wednesday

I wish I were one of those women who doesn't eat when she's stressed. Unfortunately, the more frazzled and frustrated I feel at GLC, the more I put in my mouth to cheer myself up. I ate far too much when we eventually got out of bed and went for our Chinese, ordering myself a banquet and then finishing Liz's leftovers. The next day was particularly bad. I made myself a healthy lunch before I left the house: superfood salad with seeds. But I couldn't resist a choc-chip brioche and leftover piece of tarte tatin for breakfast. Mid-morning Mike annoyed me so much, I caved in and had one of the doughnuts Abbe had brought in for her birthday. Then I ate my healthy lunch at my desk at twelve, then at one when the sandwich guy arrived I bought my favourite: smoked salmon baguette with dill butter. By two, Sunna phoned in despair about the latest directive from Penelope, and I snatched half an hour to go to the pub with her. I had my usual vodka and Slimline tonic with an enormous bag of crisps. We were supposed to be sharing them, but Sunna was talking too much to eat more than two crisps, so I ended up wolfing them down.

"I'm off on holiday to Cuba with him!" she was cackling.

"But you only met him a month ago?"

"I know, but I've got tons of annual leave I've got to take or I'll lose it. Plus the sex is amazing. The one good thing about working the way we do – I can afford decent holidays. He offered to pay, but it changes things, doesn't it? I don't like to feel like the little kept woman."

"I've got that restructure meeting this afternoon."

She was suddenly full of concern, all her news forgotten, "Babe. I'm so sorry. You going to be OK?"

"I'll have to be."

Bless Sunna. Like Dennis, she understood that employers would not necessarily treat you well, and that there was an approach that involved standing together which gave a disparate band of down-trodden staff a chance to negotiate a better deal than was possible individually. I had a little glimmer of insight, as I sat there feeling grateful that I at least had an ally in Sunna. "Penny sort of keeps us separate, doesn't she? As soon as we start working together and supporting one another, she picks us off with bribes and punishments. But there are more of us than there are of her."

"There's my bolshy," Sunna grinned at me. "Don't let the bastards get you down."

I had my smoked salmon sandwich as a mid-afternoon pick-me-up, along with a hot chocolate with squirty cream from the canteen. I was constantly frantic with worry, and no amount of comfort eating could make up for the fact that I hated my day-to-day existence.

At three o'clock, I went to open up the meeting room but found Mike had beaten me to it. The whole of Shared Services trooped in, as if to the gallows.

Everyone was so silent you could hear the air conditioning. I had set out individual tables like desks at school, so that I could give each person a copy of the committee paper.

"If we all look through it step by step," I explained to the gathered crowd of staff from across Shared Services, "It'll keep it very clear." I wanted them to feel I was supporting them as much as possible.

Leigh was in tears. She was huddled over her copy like it was an exam she was definitely going to fail. Jason was nowhere to be seen. He'd rung in sick the morning after the work drink and hadn't been back. It was unlike him.

I had been rehearsing what I was going to say so many times, I knew it by heart. It still made me feel nauseous, though: the anger, the guilt, and the shame.

PEOPLE PERSON

It was interesting that Mike was there but Penny wasn't. I didn't know why Mike had wanted to tag along, considering he had made it clear that he wouldn't be doing anything useful towards the restructure and I was on my own in delivering the bad news. But he had mastered the art of looking busy. Presumably if he could tell Penny he was in the meeting with me, he would be able to give the impression he had done some work on the restructure. I didn't think he'd even read the committee report, but at least at this meeting we would all go through the changes together.

I knew the report inside out. I'd chased Mike for the figures he'd used to decide that was the number that we couldn't afford, but he'd fobbed me off so many times I couldn't be bothered. Twelve posts to be cut. Twelve people would lose their jobs. We would have to agree how those twelve would be chosen. It was horrible, but the least I could do for them was make sure it was open and everyone had the chance to say how they thought it should be done.

Managing a team of staff is similar to the sports teams I used to captain. You've got to know the individual players and help them use their strengths to overcome their shortcomings. I enjoy it and my team trusts me. The only downside is that the wider department, particularly the layers of management above me, are purely political. They don't seem to contribute much to the hard work of the department, but you can bet they all know how to justify their positions in the all-important meetings with the heads of other departments and with the Board.

It's all run according to who is "up" and who is "down," meaning who is in or out of favour with Penelope and her henchwomen. I guess as I don't play the game, I'm always going to be on the side that gets pushed around.

"OK, guys," I began, "It's not good news, so I'll just come out and say it. The paper we're looking through today basically states that we are to lose twelve posts by the end of the year."

There was a collective squeak.

"Twelve?" Leigh checked, then it was Kimba's turn to burst into tears.

"That's right. Everyone is in the pool apart from me and Mike because our jobs are so different. All of you who are affected can decide, today, whether you'd rather be interviewed for a job in the new structure, or we can do a paper exercise to look at things like sickness, performance, and choose who stays and who goes that way."

There was a slight babble of conversation while those sitting at the desks absorbed these options.

"You can also elect someone to come to these meetings and ask awkward questions," I raised my voice over the hubbub. I breathed, trying not to let them see my true feelings about all this. "And don't hold back. Ask as many difficult questions as you want. Make me sweat."

There was some weak laughter at that. Melanie turned to those nearest her and said, "I don't want us to be chosen by sickness record, do you?"

"No," someone agreed.

"Interviews sound fairer, don't they?" she continued, looking to those on her other side.

There was a general murmur of assent for interviews.

Leigh raised her hand. "Who would be on the interview panel?"

I said, "we'd have to decide that – "

But then Mike piped up, "Myself, Rupert from Treasury and perhaps Louise."

I spun wildly towards him. "Wha – ? I beg your pardon?"

"Oh, did I not update you?" Mike said in an undertone, "Soz, Louise, soz."

"Why Rupert?" I asked him, as professionally as I could.

"We need someone independent," Mike breezed.

"But he's part of the affected depart – oh, well, we can discuss it later," I spat. "But I definitely need to be on the panel, Mike." I was cursing Mike inwardly. I couldn't believe he had waited till the middle of the consultation meeting to tell me this. He'd done it on purpose so I couldn't object.

I was furious, but I couldn't let my team think the managers weren't all singing from the same hymn sheet. I took a deep breath and carried on. "So, interview panel to be confirmed, is it interview you all want to go with?"

General nodding. My team were young and keen; they didn't have years of service and were familiar with interviews to demonstrate merit. I had thought they would prefer that to the impersonal matrix approach, where they would be disempowered.

"And shall we have Dennis to represent us?" Leigh asked the group.

A resounding 'yes' this time. Good. Dennis had the experience to make sure the team were given all they were entitled to. He was neither sycophantic to managers nor interested in his own glory.

"So, looking through the detail of the restructure," I began, returning to my rehearsed speech, "If you could all turn to page two, you will see the new structure chart."

Bang. The door flew open and hit the wall. We all jumped.

It was Carly, her eyes shining with triumph. She had an armful of stapled committee papers. Her entrance was giving her the attention she was transparently aiming for.

"Have you made the announcement yet?" she breathed at Mike.

Mike looked blank.

"Announcement?" I growled, furious at this interruption.

Carly was still looking at Mike, making an enormous effort to ignore me. "You know, the decision by the Board last night?"

Mike was slowly turning red as a beetroot, "I…er…I forgot." He turned to me but couldn't look me in the eye. "I'm sorry," he mouthed, sounding so mortified, I actually felt bad for him.

I wanted to take back control of the meeting but without the information, it was a farce. The sea of faces, my worried staff sitting at desks, each looking more and more confused and upset. The meeting had been disrupted to such an extent, by now they didn't know who to trust or what to believe.

Carly saw her opportunity and gave out her stack of papers, handing a bundle to the front of each row and getting them to pass copies back. "The report Louisa gave you is now out of date," she announced, brimming with importance, "Page two of this one shows the agreed new structure chart for Shared Services."

"How many fewer posts?" I asked, praying my hunch was wrong.

Carly sighed and took a moment to savour knowing more than the rest of us. "Eighty four," she said.

There was general panic then. Eighty four redundancies? There were only a hundred and twenty people working in the entire department. Two out of every three employees were going to lose their jobs. I grabbed a copy of the new report and flicked frantically to the chart.

Mike's post was safe. The whole of his Treasury team were still there, but my team had been decimated. My own post –

"It says 0.8?" I said, incredulously.

"That's right," Carly said, in mock-apologetic tones, "To meet our savings, you're going to have to work part-time."

I looked at Mike, my mind racing, "Presumably for less money, I'm going to be expected to do less? Or are you asking me to do the same job in four days instead of five?"

Mike gave me one of his grins of inane optimism, "You'll fit it all in somehow, Tiger."

We gave up the meeting as a bad job and agreed to reconvene the next day. To catch up, it looked like I was going to have to work late, so some of us clubbed together and ordered a pizza, which we shared around six o'clock, but then the computers crashed due to a generator failure, which we were clearly not meant to attribute to the previous quarter's corner-cutting where the equipment and staff had been squeezed for savings. I was so stressed about all the work we'd lost, I dashed home to Liz and we ordered a huge curry.

Sitting on our threadbare sofa, we were trying to watch last night's Eastenders I'd recorded, but I could hardly see what was on the screen. I was preoccupied and couldn't stop going back through the day's events in my mind.

I could vaguely hear Liz's voice. My mind was so filled with worries, she seemed to be far away.

"...but you could just quit," she was saying. I fought to concentrate. How long had she been talking to me for? She was looking at me with real concern. I realised I was clenching my teeth. "You know, we could just go back to being poor and happy," she was saying. "Why not? It doesn't matter."

"You don't understand," I mumbled, trying to relax my jaw. *Ouch.* I had clearly being holding my whole face and neck in such a tense sort of position, unlocking it had resulted in a dull throbbing headache. "I *have* been looking. There are no decent jobs around at the moment. Swinton just doesn't have many well-paid professional roles, and how many employers can you think of? GLC is my only hope."

She gave me a tired smile. "Perhaps you're right," she soothed. "Maybe we should just put up with it for another year or so, and save up as much as we can."

I couldn't tell Liz about the pay-cut I was being forced to take. I knew her first thought wouldn't be for herself anyway, but for little Joseph. Without the disposable income I had on top of our rent and bills, I would be in much less of a position to help Amanda out with cheques here and there. Unless we downsized and found an even tinier flat that we currently shared, or one further out of town, perhaps in grimy Dene, so that our journey to work became a gruelling commute. But I wouldn't ask Liz to do that, even though I knew she would agree. Our quality of life was low enough. And I was the breadwinner, goddamnit. I was going to make a decent amount of money for the woman I loved.

I ate a tub of ice cream while we waited for our delivery to arrive, fretting about how long it would take my team to make up for all the hours of work we'd lost today. When the curry came, I ate all mine and finished Liz's leftovers as well as the stack of complimentary poppadoms. After half a bottle of Bailey's in front of the television, I was falling asleep, stuffed and bloated, but still on permanent high alert.

Chapter Eight

Thursday

I was involved in the interviews where my team had to compete for the few jobs left in the new structure. The youngest took it the hardest, coming to my office and crying, saying how hard they were finding the whole situation. I felt like crying too, but kept steely cold: my face like a mask. "It's not personal," I kept saying. But with Penelope, of course, it always was personal. If I'd been a bit more diplomatic, bitten my tongue and fitted in a bit better, she wouldn't have done this to teach me a lesson. But I had to speak my mind, I just *had* to. I wondered if my team would forgive me if they ever found out.

They had opted for our only remaining union rep, Dennis, as their spokesperson and their independent champion who would ensure the proper process was followed.

Dennis was one of the few black people we had working at GLC. In a uniformly white area like Swinton, it must have been pretty lonely for black families. At my school up the road, I can't remember a single black pupil; we were small-town Southerners with only maybe a handful of kids who weren't born and bred in Swinton or a surrounding suburb. As an adult who couldn't afford to move away, I was learning that Swinton's politics ran along the lines of quiet, risk-averse suburban values, suspicious of the new and the fancy.

In my early days when I had done more "personnel" work in a retail setting, I had tried to improve the situation. It bothered me that we had a high proportion of black people applying for jobs at the boutique I first worked for and later, Sainsbury's, but not getting them. I used to coach managers in how they might be subconsciously discriminating, particularly when it got to the interview stage and they could see the race of the candidates in front of them. No amount of anonymised application forms seemed to be able to shake the Swinton-bias.

Now that I managed a team, I felt it was my duty to do as much as I could to make sure black and Asian people could work at GLC and get the promotions they deserved. For brilliant exceptions like Sunna, I felt like she had done enough already and it was too much of a burden to expect her to also sort out the casual racist bias at her workplace. I figured it was white people who were causing the problem, so it was down to me as a white person to resolve it.

In these days of HR, equal opportunities had been sublimated into something strategic, and our diversity had never been worse. In fact, you only succeeded at GLC if you were a clone of the management board. Within the HR department, your face needed to fit with Penelope. Perfectly well-qualified and suitable people of all backgrounds couldn't get in.

Dennis was from London, like Sunna. He was, however, an old fashioned trade union rep and it was quite amazing that he was still at GLC. He had worked there forever, remembering the place when it had been Council-run, and maybe even Penelope didn't relish the potential fight on her hands if she sacked a man who was in several minority groups. I'm not saying she was *racist*, exactly, but Dennis rubbed her up the wrong way for so many other reasons: he spoke his mind, he was proud that his family had always been working class, he didn't suffer fools. He was big and a man's man and pointed out flaws of powerful people who weren't used to being challenged. He seemed to see through some of the management spin and would ask awkward questions about proposals. There was also the fact that he was extremely hard-working and good at his job.

I loved it when Dennis came to the pub with us all, although at meetings like this one, being on the opposing side to him, he was hard to argue with. He was a proper philosopher, coming out with the most incredible counter-culture pronouncements and displaying incredible strength of character in the face of all-pervading opposition. GLC management, which included most of the HR department, hated him and took no trouble concealing their contempt. They said publicly that Dennis was a dinosaur, that trade unions were outdated and obstructive, and that now HR had come along to save the day, staff shouldn't need trade unions for anything unless they just wanted to make trouble and refuse to come to work over the most piffling objections about health and safety.

At the meeting the day before, with the restructure looming and hundreds of jobs to go, he had been a formidable opponent.

He didn't read from any notes but just began to speak. Dennis was always stoic, his calm tone of voice belying the fire of his beliefs. "Ordinary people came to work for GLC many years ago, and they've been working hard, doing their jobs all that time, day in, day out, and now you spring this on them. Most I've spoken to have planned their family's finances around working at GLC till retirement. If they lose their jobs ten years earlier than they'd thought, it's very difficult to get something else at that age. But they can't afford not to have that income coming in, plus their pensions are going to be short by ten years of contributions. What would you do in their situation, Penelope?"

Penny had been equally unflappable, but rather than fiery with purpose like Dennis, her voice was ice cold. "The organisation can't concern itself with that, as you know. If savings aren't found, the danger is that GLC won't be in business in ten years' time. Then all employees have lost their incomes, and their *pension contributions.*" She was icy in her sarcasm. "To put your question back to you, Dennis – what would you do?"

"You knew this financial crisis was coming," he continued, not missing a beat. "You and your senior management colleagues have been happy to take the credit for profits over the time we have operated as a private company, but what you failed to report was that the finances were not sustainable and you were stealing from future years. Why didn't GLC save up for this difficult time in advance? I wouldn't have paid the Board their bonuses for the last three years."

"Well, that would have been naïve, to say the least."

"Don't bite the hand that feeds, eh, Penny?"

"In any case, the Board were presented with a number of options, as you know, and this restructure is the one they went for. There were alternatives with considerably fewer redundancies, but this was their preference."

"Only obeying orders, then? That's your defence?" Dennis seemed warm and father-like, even when scoffing. I thought about how much I missed my dad.

"Dennis, this restructure is not up for discussion," Penny snapped. "Your role is to ensure the staff understand the process, as they seem to have opted for you to represent them."

"Oh, that's good consultation, that is!" Dennis laughed. "At this stage the redundancies are only supposed to be proposed. Staff are supposed to have the chance to put forward alternatives, as you know. And you're supposed to consider them sensibly."

"Have you got any alternative suggestions?" Penny smiled icily at the staff. Most of them looked too despondent to even be keeping up with the conversation. Jason might have had the brains to ask some questions, but he still wasn't back from sick leave. I supposed he had been cowed by that idiot Rupert, a thought which made me inwardly fume. I couldn't publicly object to what was happening – I had to give the impression that I was in agreement. It was the only professional thing I could think of to do in the circumstances.

"Just to say that I have set up a counselling service for all GLC staff now," I murmured. I can't get you guys jobs but I can give you someone to offload onto, I thought. Jesus, what had I become?

"Well, then," Penelope beamed in shark-like triumph. "All that remains is for us to agree the method of selection for redundancy."

"What about redeployment?" Dennis wanted to know.

"There are such efficiencies to be had in the new structure that there are no suitable vacancies of similar work for those displaced."

Displaced? She meant people losing their jobs. In a town like Swinton, the alternatives were to work in a shop for considerably less money and security, or move away.

I was waiting for her to announce that our jobs would be fought for against outsiders. I couldn't raise this myself because I hadn't officially been told, and didn't want to admit to hacking into Mike's emails.

But she didn't mention it and within a half hour meeting she had mapped out how she would meet her savings by decimating my team and several others, and how an interview process would decide who would be the lucky few to keep their jobs. As she swept out of the room, I could have sworn I felt the temperature rise a little, as if the icy feeling in the meeting had emanated from her.

Chapter Nine

I couldn't bring myself to tell Liz what I was having to do at work. I knew she would hear about it soon enough, but for the first few evenings I said nothing. If she could tell that I was miserable, she didn't press me for an explanation. Just looked after me and was her own wonderful self. But I couldn't return the love. I was numb.

I dragged myself into work each day, no matter how much I wanted to flee from this awful responsibility. You can't make it a pleasant experience, being selected for redundancy, but you owe it to the people going through it to treat them with respect and be honest with them. If I wimped out and refused to administer the massive restructure, I knew there were plenty of GLC hopefuls who would grab the opportunity to impress Penelope by doing it in my absence, and they wouldn't be nearly so kind about it.

I went into the meeting room we were using for the interviewing, and was irritated to find Mike and Rupert in there already, laughing and full of laddy bonhomie. I sort of cleared my throat as I sat down, but they carried on talking and completely ignored me. I made a show of organising my papers and tapped them on the desk to suggest we should get going.

No response.

So much for the subtle approach. "Guys," I said, with as much authority as I could muster. "We need to prepare. The first person will be here in less than ten minutes."

They reluctantly turned in their seats to look at the packs of paperwork I'd brought them. The pair of them: Mike short, Rupert lanky, looked for all the world like a couple of overgrown schoolboys with a boring teacher. Mike flicked through the pack and said, "I'm going off-piste with this, Louise."

"What do you mean?" I growled.

"Well, all this – " He ran his thumb down the pages making a *thr-pp* noise. "It's overkill, isn't it, really. I'll just ask a couple of questions and leave it to instinct."

No, you bloody won't. "The only problem with that, Mike, is you've got to ask all the candidates the same questions, and it's hard to remember what you've asked if you've ad-libbed. You get inconsistency without meaning it."

"I'm going to ask them what animal they are most like," Rupert smirked. "That kind of off-the-wall question gets used all the time in cutting-edge businesses."

"What kind of answer would we be looking for?" I spat. "How precisely would you measure how well someone had answered that? And given how sensitive this situation is, don't we run the risk of making the candidates think we're not taking this seriously?"

Rupert looked ready to argue but when he saw Mike crumple into hen-pecked silence, he shut up as well. I didn't know whether to be pleased at being assertive or lament my being able to give withering feedback that cowed grown men; a bit of both, probably.

Leigh poked her head around the door. "Should I come in? The letter said nine thirty...."

"Of course, of course," Mike breezed, jumping up to welcome her in. I'll say this for him, he may be useless but he can be kind in a fatherly sort of way.

She sat down opposite the three of us, looking very young and very scared.

I started. "Now, we're saying the same to everyone. This is a normal interview, just like you did when you got the job here. Just try and relax if you possibly can. There's no trick questions, just show us what you know, and pretend we don't know anything about what you do – tell us everything."

"OK," Leigh gulped. "So, I should treat you like strangers?"

"Exactly. Rupert here is from the Finance team, so you can assume everything you're telling him about the Resourcing work you do is news to him. You know Mike, but he doesn't get too involved with the day-to-day, so again, tell him everything you do. Now, I know from experience how hard it is to be interviewed by someone you know, particularly your manager, but at least you've got one familiar face and if you struggle, I'd recommend looking at the other two and pretending I'm not here."

"Gotcha." She was able to smile slightly now. I'd deliberately lengthened my spiel for Leigh, to give her a chance to calm down. I remembered she'd been a nervous wreck at the original interview, and had needed to get beta blockers prescribed by her doctor to get her through her driving test. Any situation where she thought she was being scrutinised and assessed, she went to pieces.

Rupert kicked off with the general questions I'd written for him about her current job. This allowed her to open up and genuinely explain her duties to someone who didn't know what they were. She gabbled her way through, shaking and unable to make eye contact, but at least she was getting the marks for saying the right things. Next, Mike asked a couple of scenario questions I'd put together, where she had to explain how she would deal with a complaint and an error made on the computer system. She was able to go onto autopilot then because this was stuff she did every day, she knew it and she was proud of it. Finally I asked her the equal opps question and asked her if there was anything she wanted to ask us.

Leigh blushed scarlet and looked down at her hands. In a small voice she said, "...supposing I went off on maternity leave quite soon, how would that affect...?"

"If anything it would help you," I said quickly. "We would make every effort to place a pregnant women in a role if there is one. And you're not obliged to tell us – "

"You're pregnant?" Mike bellowed over me.

I raised my hand to stop her but she had already nodded yes.

"We're going to pretend you haven't told us that, but you get some advice and decide what you want to do," I urged, "The last thing I want is for you to go away thinking that you might not get a role because you're pregnant, that would get us into very hot water." I said this last to Mike with a look that meant, *don't even think about it.* Then I ended the interview and Leigh scuttled gratefully out of the room.

"Pregnant," Rupert spat. "Silly little cow. We've got to make savings, how can we justify paying her wages for a year when she's not there?"

"And paying for someone to cover the post?" Mike mused, looking worried.

"It's not worth it, lads," I said over them both. "I don't know whether she is pregnant already or just trying," I bluffed, "but if she brings in the doctor's note showing she is, we'd be best just slotting her in to a job in the new structure." I didn't add that if they tried anything funny with Leigh, I'd offer her free HR advice myself.

"But then we have to spend more on even fewer staff!" Mike shrieked.

I couldn't quite believe he was thinking about lovely Leigh as a potential problem: a pregnant woman who we couldn't make redundant. I suppose that is how I am meant to think but I just can't do it. She was so young and I wasn't sure how Jason felt about her – that's assuming the baby was his. She had looked so scared in the interview. She would really need her job now, and so would Jason if he was going to be a dad. I resolved to step out of my HR role for five minutes and chat to Leigh as soon as I got a chance. I was more interested in making sure she got what was best for her than protecting the company.

I suppose it was then that I realised that I couldn't give a shit about my job any more.

Chapter Ten

Monday

At first I was really strict about only going in to the office Monday to Thursday. The company had screwed me over and they were making a saving based on me working only four days a week. I wasn't getting paid for Fridays after all, so the first three-day weekend was a nice novelty. I did things to relax, activities I hadn't dreamed of when I had been working such long hours. I went to the local swimming pool, I hit the shops, I caught up with my friend Vicky who's a full-time mum.

But I couldn't lie to myself for long.

I had to admit that I was spending my unpaid, home-alone Fridays stressing about everything I hadn't done at work. So very soon I started going in on my day off, at first just for the morning, but before I knew it I was staying for the entire day. And before long I was still having to go in on Saturdays as before, just because it was a quiet time when my team weren't in asking me questions. So I was soon working six days a week like always but this time I was only being paid for four.

Jason had phoned in sick that morning, very unlike him, and I found myself run ragged trying to do his work, too.

I could feel myself getting sick long before it happened. I was working stupid hours and had found myself unable to sleep, at all, for three nights straight. Sunna had looked at me in alarm over our Friday lunch and said, "Either you go and tell that excuse for a manager that you need some help, or I am going to call you an ambulance. You choose."

So I went to see Mike. As professionally and positively as I could, I told him about how overloaded I was at the moment. I suggested some solutions I'd come up with to get it all done but needed his approval to cut some corners on less important projects, unless he could help me get some more time on at least one of them. I didn't point out that his unilateral change to our turnaround times meant we had been firefighting. I didn't tell him that the one time Liz and I had actually booked a romantic city break, I had had to cancel it to come in to work over the entire weekend. Some things are not exactly diplomatic.

Mike sat there with his inane over-confident grin, presumably listening, although if I didn't know better I'd say he looked like a very relaxed person waiting for a slightly irritating noise to come to an end. When I stopped talking, he waited a couple of seconds, then got up and walked around his desk. To my horror, he put a fatherly arm round my shoulders.

"Oh, Louise, Louise, Louise," he chanted, rocking me from side to side. "What-are-we-going-to-do-with-*you*?" He said it like some sort of playground skipping rhyme, rocking me back and forth with each syllable.

It was disturbing but I needed him on board, so I laughed like this was a great management response to an overworked employee. Mike chuckled, strolled back round to his chair, and sat himself down again.

He arched his fingers over his bloated belly and sat back with his little grin. He was proud of always being calm under pressure. He was always calm because he never knew what the hell was going on.

"Let me ask you something, Louise," he sighed. He had that patronising father-like tone again, "Did you get paid last month?"

What? "Er...yes, I did."

"And do you believe that you'll get paid next month?"

"Sure." I could see where this was going.

Mike gave me a little wink. "Then everything that happens in between is 'detail,' and I don't do detail."

I let out a groan. Another brilliant Mike-ism.

"Now get back out there, Tiger," he said, standing up behind his desk to get me to leave, "and don't worry so much." And with that, he mentally ticked me off his to-do list and returned to his screen, furrowing his brow as if he was poring over performance stats rather than the dating site I knew he was looking at.

I left Mike's office before I said something rude to him. I had asked for help but it was just not going to come.

So I did whatever it took to survive. My mental and physical health in tatters, I never felt myself being gradually corrupted. My values were eroded so gradually that I honestly never noticed how differently I was behaving. I had the odd queasy moment, like over the breaks for the night workers.

I don't know what I was expecting. Don't forget, HR is the profession that has decreed that human beings can rest by doing a different kind of work.

I went straight from my pointless meeting with Mike to the outer office that flanked Penelope Ross's office door. I was not only working part-time now, I also had far fewer members of my team so we had all taken on extra work. I was getting more involved with rotas for GLC staff, and it was that that I needed to discuss with Penny.

She had had her outer-office area redecorated on arrival, I knew, and the bright colours of her own Boden-outfits were very much in evidence. The walls were turquoise, the skirting boards and window sills a contrasting lemon-yellow. The lampshade, carpet and the oversized vases were emerald green. It did make for a holiday feel, ironically enough considering how stressed Penelope's staff tended to feel as they sat there waiting for her.

Carly sat behind the desk chatting to me and answering the phone in her confident, professional manner. She had one of those voices that female TV presenters have, you know the kind, the inflection is very exciting, engaging and personable.

Carly was one-half of Penelope's PA. She had been recruited as the job-share partner for Hazel when Hazel returned from having her second baby. Hazel, I knew, was having problems with post-natal depression. I had always liked Hazel: she made time to be nice even when she was rushed off her feet. The second half of the week, when Carly would be the one in the outer office that protected Penelope from the hoi polloi, I must admit I would find excuses not to go in there.

Immersing myself in Carly's world for a few moments was my attempt to forget my own racing worries. The PA also had to deal with stray people who had got lost within the GLC offices. Some of the social housing work was charity, really, aimed at helping some really vulnerable people to get back on their feet. An occasional Eastern European family might be bussed in from an overflowing London borough and would be forced to integrate with a hostile estate of Swinton's least welcoming. Rupert had ensured that GLC took advantage of central government funding schemes to run what would otherwise be a loss-making service, so in fact we were all benefiting from a profit at the taxpayer's expense. I could never understand how a bureaucratic hand-out could form part of a supposedly lean and efficient business model but was glad we gave something back to less fortunate folk, as otherwise GLC seemed to be a relentless force against the everyday family. Newcomers, especially anyone who could be possibly be seen as foreign or an asylum seeker, were treated extremely callously by Swinton folk who liked to consider themselves good Christians.

There are some GLC employees who have so narrowly avoided the life of poverty that you might think they would show some compassion to the unfortunates who presented themselves. Carly was one of these, but compassion was not a word you would associate with her.

A woman in leggings and a long tattered t-shirt was sobbing in front of the desk. I was trying not to get involved, but Carly's whole manner made me feel quite ill.

In between phone calls Carly spat, "Your mistakes are not my problem. If you have made poor life choices, you will have to live with them."

The woman would wave a piece of paper, gesticulate, babble words that were foreign to my ears but peppered with English, such as "running away from him," "children" and "you please help us, Madam," and Carly surveyed her with smug pity, utterly determined not to understand.

After a final phone call during which Carly said, "absolutely, Penny, darling," at least four hundred times, Carly hung up and gave me a patronising smile like some kind of well-groomed crocodile. "You can go in now," she squealed.

I rushed in and stammered out my questions, very aware that I mustn't waste a second of the boss's time. She already had the exasperated look she saved for underlings who dared to ask for clarification of one of her more breath-taking tortures for GLC staff.

My questions centred around some change management I was doing for her, relating to the staff rotas I now found were part of my job description. The GLC night wardens had always been paid for their breaks because management recognised that with only one of them on shift, managing a depot each, they might sit down with a coffee in the office, but the phone would ring. Other night staff might come in with a problem and emergencies would still happen. They could have done with a proper old-school Union rep like my dad to fight their corner, because the HR department had identified them as a soft target and had plans to find some cost savings by squeezing some more work out of them. As my dad would have said: if the organisation is paying for someone to be there, it's because there is work to be done. The night worker would be on shift for hours in the night, working hard, and had always looked forward to a fifteen minute sit down with a cuppa which may or may not be interrupted. They weren't paid a fortune and the workloads had steadily increased over the years. These days, with no money to put a second worker on shift as back-up, a "break" would tend to be snatched in five minute pockets and didn't allow for leaving the building. There was nowhere to go at maybe 1am, and being able to make a personal call wasn't exactly a useful perk at that time.

So the breaks were paid. This cost GLC about twenty pounds per night. Not a fortune.

But Penelope needed to be seen to make savings, with clever ideas for "efficiencies," and she didn't want the hassle of going after the powerful expensive staff. So this group of mostly unseen workers were to be leaned on. Their breaks were to become unpaid. If they wanted to sit down with a cuppa, they would have to pay for the time out of their pay checks.

Penny had actually given this project to Mike, but he had seen that it might involve effort and conflict and had quickly delegated it to me. Mike had told me that it would be "a good project for my development," if I told the night wardens myself.

I checked with Penelope what the message was.

"So the breaks could still be taken, but from now on the staff would not be paid for the time."

"Yes."

"Would there be relief staff?"

"No."

"Would the night workers be able to take the phone off the hook for a few minutes?"

"No."

"Could they pop home, those that lived close enough?"

"No."

"Could they stand outside and smoke, maybe sit in their cars?"

"Nope."

"Louisa," Penelope sighed, her voice suggesting that she was explaining a very simple concept to a child who was wilfully refusing to understand. "Let me be *quite* clear. Breaks should be unpaid. We are merely introducing the consistency that should always have applied. We are very happy for the night-workers to take a well-earned break. We are simply asking that they be flexible should an emergency occur during that break."

Meaning, of course, that their "break" from work might be filled with some work to do.

George Orwell would have been proud of this one.

The message I had to deliver may have been unfair and unpopular, but I didn't want to avoid a difficult part of my job. What I needed was a role model, someone to imagine when I went into battle. I certainly couldn't picture Mike having to see through a difficult task like this. He would weasel out of it, as in fact he had, "delegating" the role of messenger to me. I would rather be brave and unpopular than take the line of least resistance.

Before my meeting with Penny I had done my homework. I could not go in and speak to her without coming up with my own strategy for how to deal with this. I had asked myself, what would Sunna do?

Sunna always liked to get things clear in her own mind before she enforced it with her customers. I admired her style. She would never say, "I don't agree with this, but Penny says we've got to..." Without fail, Sunna would always find a way to square the latest edict in her head. She looked for the sense in it and then delivered the message with strength. I loved her for her integrity, but scarily, Penelope would often refer to Sunna as "on message." I had asked Sunna to talk me through this one, and with the two of us looking resolutely at the positives, she had sort of helped me to accept this unpaid breaks change by saying, "you can bet the night workers take longer than their fifteen minutes to make up for the interruptions. That's what I'd do."

PEOPLE PERSON

I never knew whether or not what she was saying was right, but she made me feel calm enough about the change to do my job and be professional. Thanks, Sunna. How would I get through this shitty job without you?

I looked at Penelope, sitting behind her big heavy wooden desk. I tried not to let the disgust show on my face. She didn't look much like the stereotypical evil boss. I glared at her trendy tousled hairdo, her fresh no-make up look, and wondered whether anyone who met her on the street could believe what vicious behaviour she was capable of. The woman was ruthless. I cleared my throat to ask another question, and noted with alarm the increasing impatience appearing on that immaculate face. "So... we are simply asking that the staff be flexible should an emergency occur during that unpaid break," I parroted.

"*Correct*," she breathed. The sarcasm was cutting.

"And an emergency would be...?"

"Any work that needs dealing with," Penny gave the tiniest suggestion of a grin. She looked terrifying.

"They have to do any work that comes in, on their own time, unpaid?" I couldn't keep the sense of injustice out of my voice, "And when their break is over, they go back to work, even if they've spent their entire break working."

"Louisa." Penny's voice was starting to climb to a dangerous level. "I really do not have the time to sit here going through your project in such a level of detail. This is your responsibility and I need to get on to many other far more significant pieces of work..."

"Yes, yes, understood, Penelope," I said quickly, and made for the door. "I appreciate your time for this coaching."

Outside her office door, I breathed.

It was about the seductive power of influence. If I had to justify my appalling behaviour, I would say that there are few professions outside teaching and nursing where I could have an interesting role, not just be assisting a man. Most of the jobs my friends do seem to involve a male boss, a guy who is in charge, and the girls seem to be implementing his decisions. But in Human Resources, people expect you to be female. Think about it, most other jobs you go in to, you have to fight a little bit, as a girl, don't you? But for some reason, HR is made up of a high proportion of female staff and managers. I had actually felt like I could be myself, at least to start with.

When you get to my level, the intoxicating pull was all about getting the leader to make a decision that affects others, and feeling powerful, but if I was honest, you didn't have to learn the maturity or the judgement of being a leader yourself. Penelope represented us all, a modern-day Lady Macbeth, and the CEO was doing what she said, enacting Penny's power-crazed schemes.

The environment she created was terrifying in its competitive back-biting. Put simply, I feared for my job every single day. Being at work I had to constantly jockey for position with colleagues who would sweetly run me down or capitalise on some tiny flaw.

Worse still was when I would dare to go home and the anxiety of not being at work, and the anxiety of the things that were being said about me while I wasn't there, were even more stressful. If I could drop off to sleep at all I would wake throughout the night with horrible guilt at something I hadn't managed to do, imagining the snide repercussions of those around me at work.

Carly was giving me a supercilious look, as if me leaning against Penny's door and getting my breathing back to normal wasn't a common sight in the Director's outer office. Instead of what I would have liked to say to Carly I sang out, "Perfect, got all the information I need, thanks *so* much for getting me some time with Penelope, Carly." It didn't hurt to be nice.

If my confidence wrong-footed her, she never let on. "No probs," she called, phoney and bitchy in equal measure. I marched off to the door back to the corridor, holding my composure till I could get out of her sight. Just as I was disappearing out the door, she trilled, "oh, Louisa –"

I came back. "Carly?"

She gave me a huge grin. "You haven't forgotten about presenting the night wardens' changes in pay to the Board, have you?"

You've got to be joking – "What? Surely Penelope – "

"Oh, no, Penny thought it would be good for your development if you got that experience. Tomorrow morning, OK?"

I couldn't believe this. Ordinarily, I would jump at the chance to enhance my CV with a piece of work that should have been done at a much higher level than mine, but this was a suicide mission. The only reason Penelope could have farmed this task out to me is that she wanted to distance herself from what she had asked me to do. And with no warning of the Board meeting, I would be up all night preparing my presentation.

The hot fear in my stomach felt like food poisoning. Carly's piranha smile seemed to whirl before my eyes. *I can't. No one can do what is being asked of me. It's impossible.*

Then the still, small voice inside came to me. *If anyone can, Louisa Cannes.* Why not try? Failure wouldn't kill me, and I just might win through.

Well, come on then, I thought to myself. If that's what you have to do, then stop moaning and get on with it.

I gave Carly a relaxed smile which seemed to throw her off balance. "Perfect," I breathed, forcing my voice to brim with a confidence I could almost believe myself, "See you there."

Chapter Eleven

I hate giving presentations. Even when I'm supposed to be explaining stuff I know really well, something about standing in front of people and talking into the silence freaks me out. I imagine that the audience think I'm stupid and the things I'm saying are boring. I get embarrassed, I gabble, my legs shake, my heart seems to pound in my throat, I lose my place in my notes, and I tend to try and rush through to get the presentation finished and over with as quickly as I can.

I couldn't believe the ridiculous situation I had been placed in by the people around me. It was so unfair and many people in my position would refuse to accept it. But what was the point of complaining in a company where pointing out that Penelope and her allies were behaving like controlling bullies was punished so severely? I remembered poor Sam, who just a few months before I had been responsible for destroying. I had never thought about how she had felt until now. I could finally understand what I had put her through now that Penelope was undermining me in the same way.

It turned out Mike hadn't explained to me that the whole of his restructure plan should have been presented to the Board for their approval. It was just some internal red tape, but it could scupper all the work we had done if we did not have the right boxes ticked. The Board were notorious for their fickle attitude. You needed to sweet talk them and make sure they felt really important if you wanted them to agree to your ideas. Everyone knew that. But Mike hadn't bothered to do the preparation work to get them on side, he just expected me to tack it on to the work I had to do, to get the night wardens' pay downgrading approved. He knew I was slogging my guts out on my own project and so he just assumed I could do his dirty work at the same time.

Even though I was sacrificing my own free time, I had no choice. The better I prepared for a presentation like this, the more confident I would feel when I actually got in front of the scary Board and the less likely they would be to catch me out with one of their deliberately humiliating questions. So here I was, up all night doing the slides and rehearsing what I was going to say.

My kitchen table was covered with notes and printed out versions of the slides. Carly needed my slides so she could add it to the Board documents and load it up on the screen for me to present. I had already sent one version of my presentation to her earlier just as I was leaving work, but had since found out that there was yet more I needed to include that Mike hadn't told me about. So I planned to finish my changes, then send Carly the updated version first thing in the morning. I must have fallen asleep at my kitchen table at some point around 2am so staggered to bed and lay awake, fretting.

At first light I rushed into work. I ran round to Carly's desk to talk her through my final, revised presentation, and check she was OK to load up the right version for the Board to look at. I had thought of everything. I couldn't have worked any harder.

The Board had spent a few minutes laughing and joking with each other as Penelope sat near them in an icy silence. When they had settled they looked indulgently at me. I stood alone in front of them, gulping, my presentation notes in my hand. Mike arrived late and sat at the very back, a goofy grin on his fat face. I tried to ignore him as he had contributed nothing to my hard work but would no doubt try to take the credit if things went well. I hadn't really seen the Board before, only heard about their shadowy influence. They were made up of a number of men in their sixties and seventies, a couple of much younger men who clearly considered themselves to be hotshots, plus a couple of ladies of the posh middle-aged variety. Too nervous to take much in, all I could see was a blur of suits and steely grey hair, with the female members looking like wealthy dowagers in their pearls and elaborate hair dos.

PEOPLE PERSON

I took a deep breath and started. My butterflies were in danger of making my voice high-pitched and my hands shake, but I fought to appear calm. As I was taking the Board through my first few bullet points, I glanced at the screen where my PowerPoint slides were being clicked through for me by Carly. Mid-sentence, I gaped. My heart sinking, I realised the slides on the screen were not tallying with what I was saying. I looked at Carly in horror.

Had she deliberately loaded on the old version of the slides? Surely not. It must have been an innocent mistake. Even that little madam wouldn't do that, I couldn't believe it of her. In case there was any chance that she had just slipped up, I decided that I wasn't going to make her feel bad about it. I'm not like that. So I soldiered on, skipping through the slides that no longer made sense, and on occasion having to say, "uh, the figure in your handout is actually out of date now, the new total is..."

Sitting cosily next to Penelope, Carly had on a tight black satin pencil skirt and a pussy bow blouse, sleekly accessorised with patent heels. Personally, I can't be bothered with such fashionable workwear. A washable trouser suit from Debenham's will do me and flat boots for running around in. I must admit, the weight I've put on since I started working at GLC means I would rather pull on something comfortable and covering. The room was warm but I couldn't take off my jacket, as that would reveal that my trousers were held together with safety pins. I couldn't do up the fly at the moment.

I finished explaining Mike's plan, reducing the number of HR administrators by basically getting line managers to do some of our record keeping for us. It was the way HR was going, nothing new but new to GLC. Then I got to the stuff I really wanted to tell them about – my strategy for the year. I had various ideas for changes I wanted to bring in. I had crystallised it all into five projects I wanted agreement on. Knowing how short Mike's attention span was in my monthly one-to-ones, and wanting time to write a decent report on each project, I had worked on one a month and shown Mike each one at a different monthly supervision meeting, so he'd be in the loop and give me some support at the Board meeting. I had heard that they tended to be a cross between Dragon's Den and a Stalinist show trial.

"Any questions?" I smiled at the Board, relieved to have got through my ordeal.

Carly piped up, "Your first project you described, that sounds like just pushing the admin onto busy managers?"

I blinked. I was shocked by such a bitchy betrayal, even from her. *Whose side are you on?*

She was right of course; Mike's attention-grabbing trimming of staff meant my team had been reduced to the point we now desperately needed to minimise our paperwork, but I couldn't let the Board know that. They saw the whole of HR as obstructive pen-pushers. Administration falling to managers would never be agreed.

Several Board members gave me pitying looks. Penelope gave a slight titter in the awkward silence.

Carly smiled like a cougar spotting a bleeding gazelle.

It was bloody Mike's project any way! What did I care if it didn't get through the Board approval process? I was more interested in the other stuff I had come up with, which would actually make our service better. They seemed not to have heard that. I glanced at Mike, who sort of shrugged and looked down. I was clearly on my own.

Was I going to curl up in a ball and hope it all went away?

No.

I forced myself to think on my feet.

"What we're actually doing, Carly," I beamed, "is making use of the fact that managers make their own staffing records as a matter of course. Rather than having a clunky, centralised rival set of information, we're cutting out the duplication, and saying, 'GLC deserves up-to-date data from the coal face.'"

The Board were sitting up now. They had been programmed to get excited by words like "duplication" and "coal face."

Carly's smile had slipped slightly but she rallied quickly and went again for the jugular, "So with less admin to do, of course your team will be able to lose more posts in future."

Little witch. "Not at all," I breezed, thinking fast, "In fact, we've become as lean as possible already. My few remaining advisors will move into a far more effective role of experts to give managers a more proactive service. With less bureaucracy, we will be able to research trends, troubleshoot, and get out and help staff in the workplace, rather than be mistaken for a back office function."

Troubleshoot? Proactive? These were brilliant words that somehow earned respect when used at GLC. I was on fire.

Carly now looked as if she were chewing on a wasp. "But HR *is* a back office function," she whined, looking very put out.

Oh, no. I couldn't let that pass. In the Board's collective minds, "frontline" was good while "back-office" was bad, and ripe for merging with other organisations to save money. "*Personnel* was back-office, Carly," I treated her to my most patronising smile, "Since we became HR, the benefits we've added include...."

And then I was in the zone. I didn't need any Powerpoint notes to tell me how brilliant my team was. I reeled off facts and figures to demonstrate their success. I knew how hard they worked, so I spouted numbers of outputs at the Board and explained how many that meant each member of staff was getting through each day. I knew it was impressive and the Board members were looking more cheerful by the minute.

Finally I brought in the details of a new sickness absence policy I had cooked up. To reduce the incidents of short-term absence, GLC would no longer pay sick pay for the first few days an employee was off. This would deter people from taking a duvet day when they just didn't fancy going to work, leaving their colleagues to do their work. If you knew you would lose a day's pay and still decided you were really sick enough not to drag yourself in, you were probably pretty ill.

"How many days shall we not pay for?" a Board member wanted to know.

"Other organisations have had success with one day," I explained, "but then you run the risk of encouraging people to stay off for two or more days to 'get their money's worth.' If they've lost a day's pay, but by day two the sick pay kicks in again, they may well decide to stretch out their 'sickness.' So I'd say we need a good long period without sick pay, to make sure they're genuine."

What a hard-nosed bitch I was. When I had been consulting the union on this policy, Dennis had had a comment for me, rather than a question. He said, "Louisa, with respect, for someone young and fit without health problems, sick pay might look like an unnecessary drain on GLC's resources. But for someone unlucky enough to suffer with genuine illness, or needing an operation, that safety net is essential. Do you want to go back to the bad old days when workers would fall behind with their rent or bills because they were unlucky enough to get old and sick?"

I wish I had listened to him, but I had thought I knew it all. I was too excited by the reaction I knew I would get from the Board. As they weren't GLC employees, the policy didn't affect them at all, so they had nothing to lose. In their meeting now, they had clearly started to show off to one another with how tough they could be on the employees.

My presentation at an end, the grey haired Board became far more animated by discussing this one small part of it than they had been throughout. I think they had forgotten that I was there.

"Let's make it four days without sick pay!" one of the chaps in pin-stripes said to his cronies.

"No, five – a full week should send a message to malingerers!" cried one of the twinset-and-pearls ladies.

"Seven days!"

"Eight!"

It was like a disgusting sort of auction.

Penelope looked savagely thrilled, "So, we agree on the first eight working days without sick pay?" she purred, noting it down.

Eight days without sick pay? I was slightly nauseous at the thought. No other organisation I had researched was so mean to its staff. But the Board were keen, Penny looked ecstatic, and I was the golden girl who had made it possible. My name would be recorded as the saviour of the terrible sick pay bill, and I would be remembered for achieving savings. The holy grail of saving money.

The great thing about it was, after all their excitement, the Board approved everything I'd proposed, having only scrutinised the one small area of my paper. Brilliant. My other projects were through and my team could start working on them. It had taken me a while to get the hang of the layers of red tape at GLC, but I thought I'd cracked it this time: first get Mike's approval, then he would feed it up to Penny who would clear it with the Senior Management Team. Then Board approval, which was usually the difficult bit.

I decided that I would meet all the night workers myself to break the news about their considerably worse pay and conditions. The changes were not due to come in till the new financial year, so I had a few weeks before I would have to sit down with them all. I told myself, forget about it for now, Louisa. Enjoy a small victory before you have to deliver the shit sandwich.

When the Board were filing out and I was packing up my papers to leave, Carly slipped over and whispered, "you're welcome."

Huh? "What am I supposed to be thanking you for, Carly?"

She gave me an ingratiating grin. "I gave you those tough questions so you'd have a chance to shine. You did so well, I think I'll have to make sure I give you more challenges like that in future."

Oh, I'd heard it all, now. Her little plan to embarrass me had backfired, but she still wanted the official record to show that she hadn't been unprofessional.

"No need for that, Carly," I said, as casually as I could. "I work fine alone. I'll load up my own slides in future as well, saves confusion."

Just then, something in my head clicked. When I had said I work best alone...since when had Carly been smart enough to come up with that sort of awkward question? She had the aggression to give me a grilling, but not the brains. "Did you write those questions yourself?"

She flushed, "Actually, they came from Penny."

That didn't make any sense. I looked up at Penelope, but she had chosen that moment to sweep from the room before I could ask her anything. Had she been listening in?

But surely Penelope wanted Mike's proposal to succeed. I assumed this, because they had always presented a united front. Now I thought about it, I had always assumed that Penny thought Mike was good at his job and wanted to support him.

She didn't want to stab him in the back.

Did she?

Chapter Twelve

There was no time to make sense of Penny's actions. Rushing back to my office intending to deal with the pile of work that would no doubt have come in while I had been in the Board meeting, I nearly collided with Leigh. She had clearly been crying.

"Oh, Louisa," she said in a small voice. "I don't want to tell tales, but this has gone far enough, now."

"What's up?" I took her by the arm and gently propelled her inside my office.

"Jason's had to go into A & E this morning. He and Rupert had another fight, after a work drink. He had been trying to get better on his own at home, but he's been getting worse and he finally went to a doctor."

"*Jason?*" So that explained his first and only week off sick, and no sign of him again this morning. "He's not the sort for brawling. Is he OK?"

"He just phoned me – they've patched him up and he'll be fine if he takes it easy for a few more days. You should see his eyes, Louisa. But it's not just the physical stuff...." Leigh shivered.

I thought about this. "When you say 'fight,' is it really that the two of them decide to have a scrap, or...."

Leigh's face was pale and she had dark circles under her eyes, I noticed. "No. It's just bullying, really. Jason likes to say they got into a fight but really, Rupert just attacks him. And says all these awful things, so Jason believes he deserves it...."

I felt like there were fireworks in my chest. I fought to maintain control, "I'm glad you told me about this, Leigh," I said, using my manager voice. "I'll investigate and let you know the outcome. I'll give Jason a call now."

Once she had gone, I let myself swear. Then I grabbed the phone and called Jason's mobile. "Listen, mate, don't come in this week. You've been through enough – stay home and get some rest. I'd like to come and see you briefly, about three o'clock OK?"

Jason rented a flat not far from mine. I knew the way there from all the times I'd dropped him home after nights out with the team. The roads were clear today at three o'clock, just before the schools traffic started.

After ringing the doorbell, I stood back and looked at the little place. Leigh and Jason had recently started dating and I suppose they were the office sweethearts, and since Leigh had moved in, she worked hard to keep their two-room basement flat spotless. They had pots of lavender and sage on the doorstep, which looked scrubbed and recently whitewashed.

I heard myself gasp as the door opened. For a second, I didn't recognise the figure before me.

Jason's face was swollen and doughy, his features indistinct in the raised surface of his face. He had some egg-sized bumps coming up on his scalp, black and blue through his short hair. But worst of all were his eyes. They were entirely red – the whites were a terrifying crimson colour, and there was a dark line of bruising all around the inside of the sockets.

"Jason – " I started, my blood boiling. "Did Rupert do this to you?"

"Should have seen the state of him," Jason lisped quietly, his swollen mouth sounding thick and useless.

We went inside – Jason doing his best not to let me see how slowly he had to limp – and I made us both a cup of tea.

"Why on earth would Rupert want to do this to you?"

"Oh, there's always someone who wants to beat you up, it will always happen," Jason said, hanging his head a little. He looked ashamed. I remembered Leigh telling me he had been mercilessly bullied at school. I supposed being skinny, intelligent, and funny had made him a natural target.

"When did it happen?"

"At the end of the night, Friday night's drink – you had gone home. He kept trying to start with me." Jason's eyes were so bloodshot that looking at them was making my own eyes start to water. "I stayed till last orders with Leigh. Rupert was sitting at another table with his Treasury mates, but every time he got up to go to the bar or out the front to smoke, he'd pass our table and say something about me or Leigh. It got me really riled up. I told him to watch himself, and then he got nasty. He asked me outside, but I told him to 'F' off. I said he wasn't worth losing my good looks over."

Jason looked like a hit and run victim but was still able to crack jokes.

"Then towards the end of the night, I thought they'd gone. I couldn't see them anywhere, which was a relief if I'm honest. I didn't spot them till we had almost made it home. They were waiting for us near our flat. I don't know how they knew where we lived."

I did. The Treasury team needed everyone's pension details, which included a home address. Rupert had deliberately looked up Jason's address on the work computer system, to go round there and attack him. That was grounds for him to be in trouble on its own, never mind the savage beating he'd dished out to a colleague.

"Any witnesses?" I asked him.

"To the fight? Only Leigh, but they told her to run home or they'd make her wish she wasn't a girl, if you get what I mean." Jason paused and took a moment to calm down after saying this. Even through his injuries, he looked ready to defend her honour. "Rupert punched me a few times, then his mates held me down while he gouged my eyes, hence my Dracula impression." He gestured at his completely red eyes.

"My God. You could have lost your sight."

"S'ppose. I managed to wriggle away before he finished the job. But don't worry about it, boss. What's done is done."

"I need to look into this, mate. Colleagues can't behave like that. Who stayed longest with you in the pub?"

"Kimba and Melanie."

"...so they'd be worth talking to about Rupert coming over and trying to rattle you. Plus the bar staff might have noticed when he left and which way he went – don't they have CCTV on the pavement outside? Maybe I could get hold of the footage – "

"If you're sure you want the hassle."

My blood was boiling. I'd get that Rupert. He deserved to pay for his calculated bullying.

Jason hadn't touched his tea when I stood up to leave. I guessed his bashed up face must be too sore to drink anything hot, but I didn't want to rob him of what was left of his dignity, so didn't mention it. I had found out all I needed to, anyway.

"Jason, mate, this is a work matter, even though you don't want it to be," I said, watching his face move through alarm to resignation. "I'll speak to Mike about how we deal with it discreetly, but basically Rupert can't get away with behaving like this."

"Whatever you think, boss," Jason said, with a kind of weary gratitude, "I'll be in in the morning."

"Work from home, mate. Your eyes are scary."

I drove like a bat out of hell back to the office to catch Mike before he sauntered off home.

I burst into his office. Mike seemed to be coming round from a doze in his seat.

"Mike, Jason Mann has been assaulted by Rupert Carter-Hayes. After a work drink."

"Assaulted?" he said blearily, blinking at me like a particularly dazed guppy.

"Yes. We need to investigate and use the disciplinary policy."

That woke him up. He snapped to attention and said, "No, no we don't."

"Mike, I've seen Jason. He looks horrendous. Rupert gouged his eyes – he could have lost them."

"Nothing to do with us," Mike said shortly. "It didn't happen at work, did it?" he asked with a sudden quaver of anxiety.

"No, but it was after a work drink."

"Off the premises? Thank God." Mike settled back in his seat and folded his hands over his enormous soft belly. "Don't forget the funders' inspection in two weeks, Louise. We don't want a sniff of a scandal, not a suggestion that one of our competitors would be a safer bet. All our jobs rely on that," he said, giving me a stern look. "Does Jason want to take it further?" he asked with a second sudden panic.

"Not really, but…."

"Thank Christ! Sensible lad. He'll go far."

"I do understand," I heard myself saying. And I did, on one level. The reputational risk was significant. The timing couldn't be worse.

But.

I remembered Jason's little face as he had hung his head and said, "there's always someone to beat you up, it will always happen."

And I remembered his eyes, completely red, gouged by an attacker who had no remorse, who had lost control, wanted to annihilate and damage. A sinister young man with the crystal blue eyes who could lie so convincingly, and explain why the person he had attacked deserved it.

And make them believe it.

I could dimly hear Mike saying, "If there's no complaint, there's no crime. Nothing to investigate. Forget about it, Louise."

That was wrong, I knew it was wrong. You can't just go around beating up colleagues, there had to be consequences. I knew that Jason had had such a terrible childhood in a care home that he didn't think he deserved any better. Staff at GLC would be horrified if they knew they were working with someone who could behave in such a violent manner.

"Mike, we need to suspend Rupert, *now*. We need to find out what happened, and if he did attack Jason in the street, he should get the sack."

"Louise, think about what you're saying," Mike hissed with an angry hand movement to show he wanted me to keep my voice down. "What would an investigation entail?"

"Asking the bar staff what they saw, perhaps getting the CCTV footage from the high street."

"So GLC's name is dragged through the mud," Mike spat. "We march into a pub and say, 'we want to find out whether a GLC manager beat up a colleague.'"

"And the CCTV would have to involve the police…" I said, slowly.

"And meanwhile, you are harassing *Penelope Ross's boyfriend*," Mike practically snarled.

I noted the change of pronoun. Mike's meaning was transparent. If I insisted on doing what I knew was right, I would be on my own. He would not back an investigation.

"You're saying that if I press for proper process, Penny won't see that we have no choice? That she will actually protect her boyfriend and go against her own department's policy? That's quite a strong allegation, Mike. You're actually accusing Penelope of…" I struggled to think of the right word for what I meant. "…corruption."

"Will you stop speaking about Penelope with such disrespect?" Mike was virtually screaming with outrage, but under such painful control that it came out as no more than a whispered shriek.

I could see what would actually happen, though. If I went through with this, Penelope would make sure I found working at GLC impossible. In the same way that she had got me to get rid of Sam, she would get some hungry young thing like Carly to get rid of *me*.

And so, after some pacing around the building, chewing nervously on a large bacon and brie sandwich, I came to a decision.

I walked slowly back in to my office, not able to look my staff in the eye, knowing what I was about to do.

I phoned Jason and told him to take as long as he needed, on full pay, to get better, then to come back to work. I explained that as the incident had taken place off work premises, GLC couldn't get involved, although if Jason wanted to go to the police as a private individual I would help in any way I could. Jason's voice sounded surprised at first, then quietly defeated. "No problem, boss," he said, before he hung up.

I hated myself so much I could have thrown up.

I *was* thinking about the impact on Jason's self-esteem, but I realised that I had put my own job security above his feelings. I quickly squashed the thought. One thing I didn't think about at all, was the effect my choice would have on Jason's loyalty. I doubt that was Mike's motive, but things certainly worked out well for him.

Replacing the phone receiver with a slightly shaking hand, I swallowed hard to get rid of the nausea, and stared at the picture of Joseph. "I'm doing this for you," I whispered. "Getting money to help you is the most important thing, right?"

Chapter Thirteen

Wednesday

The next morning, I went mutinously into Mike's office for a catch-up in response to a hurried email he'd sent me. His tone had been somewhere between terse and petrified.

"The Board wants a review of all pre-employment checks," Mike was saying. He was looking sweaty and furtive, even for him.

"Why?" I asked innocently, fighting to keep my voice light. *Please not Liz.* I had been living in fear of her financial problems in the past coming to light. "Has someone been caught out? Making up a qualification they haven't got, or writing their own glowing reference when they actually got the sack for stealing?"

"Not even close," Mike responded, as I knew he would. "It's criminal records they've got excited about. A Board member received an anonymous letter saying a GLC employee has a criminal record we didn't pick up when we gave them the job."

I tried to imagine how I would react if I hadn't got Liz's court order on my conscience and feigned pragmatism. You know, a responsible manager seeking a few facts about a difficult situation. "Do we know anything about the employee? Or how serious the offence was?"

It wasn't as if we didn't have people working at GLC with past convictions. Several frontline staff I knew of had the likes of speeding, drunk driving, and minor cannabis possession charges from when they had been much younger. One woman in the Payroll team had even served time for the manslaughter of her abusive boyfriend. It had been twenty years ago when she had snapped in the face of daily domestic abuse and had had a spotless record ever since. By all accounts she was good at her job, quiet and loyal. These things didn't necessarily mean you couldn't get a job with us. It was just that we needed to know, because it was something of a calculated risk. It was always possible that you would commit the same crime again in the future, and the reputation of GLC could be in jeopardy. The local paper loved to print a story about an employee's past life to contrast with our supposed respectability. Our stakeholders were notoriously skittish in the face of any kind of scandal. Before we gave you the job, we needed the chance to consider the crime and how long ago it had been, talk to you about how you had changed your life since and get it agreed by the Board usually. They loved to play judge and jury, especially with the drug convictions. It made them feel cool to ask the new employee questions about their former shadowy life and show off to one another by using tragic slang from thirty years ago. They felt heroic by formally giving a troubled youngster a second chance.

But deliberately concealing a past conviction to get a job with us? That could never be OK. If you were prepared to lie about that, who knows what else you would be dishonest about on the job.

Mike continued, "Nope, we know nothing. But I tell you what, if it were me, I'd resign now, while there's still time. You would want to get another job, quick, before you got caught."

He was dead right. As soon as this member of staff was found out, any reference GLC gave would have to show that they had lied and were about to be sacked. Try getting another job with that on your records.

For a second, I had thought about Liz's situation and panicked. But then I told myself to calm down and think logically. A CCJ isn't a criminal record, is it? Getting into bad debt wasn't a crime, and Liz was paying it back. It didn't affect how well she could do her job, and she had never lied to anyone. And besides, she had been taken on as a contractor through an agency. This anonymous letter had definitely pointed the finger at someone working for GLC themselves. Liz couldn't be implicated.

Mike had already volunteered my team to do the donkey work to implement this audit, sifting through the old recruitment files for all our current staff, trying to find the person the anonymous letter referred to. I brought them all in on a Saturday to go through the yellowing paperwork.

The GLC buildings consist of a mismatch of old local authority buildings we had inherited, with a smattering of updated offices, and one sweeping new wing built in the last two years. Penny and the rest of the management team had given themselves light, modern new offices within the so called "leadership block" while my team were housed in a stuffy prefab which proved boiling hot in the summer and freezing cold in the winter. Part of our building was given over to archives, and the storage of files took slightly higher priority than keeping us unimportant GLC workers at a constant temperature. Damp and poorly lit, our rabbit warren of offices did little to raise morale, but Jason and I did what we could with our own money. The month before, I had brought some volunteers in with paint and rollers, and we had decorated our workplace ourselves, rather than wait for GLC to feign interest in where we spent so many hours of our lives.

Every member of my team turned-out for this particular weekend project; the pre-employment check search through the archives we had passed so many times. We were already up against it workwise, with the computer crash last week, and extra work was the last thing we needed when we were working desperately hard to catch up. I got them a load of doughnuts and promised pizzas for lunch.

I had got a random sample of recruitment files from over the last ten years. Some were still cardboard files, filled with all the documents provided at the time. Most were scanned in to the computer, where the staff had been recruited recently. The oldest few were on microfiche. I divided up the files between the people who had been able to come in on that Saturday. I took the senior appointments myself. I don't know why, but it just felt a bit wrong to have the heads of department being scrutinised like this: their salaries, home addresses, and their previous employers' performance evaluations. If it had to be done, I thought it was more appropriate if I did it myself.

I had noticed that the random sample included Rupert's recruitment, and I would be lying if I said it hadn't crossed my mind just how fantastic it would be to find him lacking in some way, if only to take him down a peg or two. I didn't really expect to find anything.

When I did, it was quite sickening.

Rupert's file fell open at a Criminal Records Bureau print-out. No offences, but a long statement of information from Swinton police in the comments box.

"Subject was questioned over an allegation of sexual assault, charges never brought. Subject claimed the alleged victim was confused due to counselling for childhood abuse and gave him mixed messages."

I had to put the file aside. Rupert had been accused of – what, exactly? Raping a girl? Then basically told her she only had herself to blame for her behaviour towards him? It sounded so similar to the way he had made Jason feel about beating him up, it put the whole sexual assault allegation in a hideous new light. Maybe the victim had never pressed charges, but I knew from my experience with the Criminal Records Bureau that they didn't include a detailed comment like that on a check unless they were very concerned about something.

Was he the one the Board had been tipped off about?

I carried on searching files. Penelope's name hadn't appeared on the random search list, but I had taken advantage of the search to get her file out, and have a good read. I saw that she had been born Penelope Ross and was not married, and had no kids. Like me, she had worked her way up from an entry level admin job. She was even younger than I realised – not forty yet.

And – according to her tenancy agreement, she had lived with Rupert for almost fifteen years.

I flicked back through Rupert's file. The CRB disclosure was dated just six years ago. He had been in a relationship with, and living with, Penelope at the time of this allegation for sexual assault. Had he attempted to force himself on another woman? Or…was Penelope the victim who had never pressed charges?

I decided to go and talk to her about it directly. I hadn't even told Mike yet – it was Saturday, after all, so I knew for sure that he wouldn't be in, but Penny would be. Besides, this one felt quite sensitive and I wanted to give her her dignity.

I sprinted over to her office, running through the empty secretarial outer office straight to her door and knocked. No Carly today, thank God. After a second I was summoned in with a curt word from inside.

PEOPLE PERSON

Penny was dressed casually for her weekend office day. She had no makeup on and the trendy hair cut was tousled artfully. She barely turned round at my arrival, her face a haughty sneer. I was clearly an unwelcome interruption.

"Penelope, I've seen a CRB check for a member of staff that concerns me," I began, as gently as I could.

She stiffened. Her face suddenly looked years younger. She looked, for a split second, like a frightened little girl. Then, just as quickly, her armour returned and she was the ice maiden again. "Oh?" she breathed, arching an eyebrow.

"It was for Rupert Carter-Hayes," I pressed on, my stomach dancing a polka. "I know how difficult this must be for you to hear since you're...ah...personally involved. But given the seriousness of the allegations, I don't know how he was cleared to work here in the first place – "

"I took full responsibility," Penny snapped. "Rupert has undergone extensive counselling and many years have passed since that time in his life. Besides, there was no conviction."

"There often isn't, with that kind of case, is there?" I asked, ensuring my voice sounded calmer than I felt. *Poor Penny.* "The victim was probably too upset, had been through enough, couldn't face him in court – "

"I see no point in discussing that particular CRB further." Her voice couldn't have been more icy if she'd dropped it into the North Sea. "Have you come across any other adverse CRB disclosures – or any other police issues?"

Oh no. Only one other in the whole audit – but I had hoped Liz's would be forgotten about in all the panic with Rupert's. "I've checked a sample of GLC employees and they were all clean. Did you want me to look at all of them? That would take a good three or four more Saturdays."

"What about agency staff, contractors?"

Damn, she was shrewd. Could I lie to Penelope? No way. She'd find out about Liz and then I'd probably be up on some sort of disciplinary charge. I'd have to be honest – but maybe I could play it down. "Just one. A CCJ for an unpaid phone bill of a few hundred pounds."

Her eyes lit up. "Which department was the member of staff in?"

I didn't like that *"was."*

"They work in IT, as a contractor. Not even a permanent member of staff. So they can't have been the one the Board member was tipped off about." *Please let it go.* "I'm pretty sure it was Rupert they were referring to."

But Penny was excited. Here was a scapegoat. Someone to sacrifice to the Board as the dodgy CRB recipient, to explain away the anonymous tip-off, and to spare Rupert.

It didn't occur to me to say that the unfortunate scapegoat was my partner. I'm not exactly honest about my personal life at GLC. None of my team would bat an eye, but the more senior members of the company have Swinton values, and being gay is seen as a slightly awkward aspect of personality. I hated to lie by omission, but it was just yet another excuse for me to be treated poorly or excluded on a social level. I had assumed that for Penny she would much rather I "didn't tell" leaving her free to "not ask".

Penny rushed off to discuss the good news with some ally or other, and I sat there like an idiot in her outer office, gloomily waiting for her. After an hour, I realised she wasn't coming back and slunk away from Carly's empty lair, praying my sense of sickening dread was wrong.

But it wasn't.

Chapter Fourteen

Monday

Just a few days later, Liz was ashen-faced at breakfast with Penny's letter in her hand.

We were sitting at our kitchen table, a few of my presentation notes still cluttering up the area where we had our porridge and snatched a few minutes together before Liz drove me in to work.

"What does this mean?" she asked, handing the letter to me. She couldn't have looked much more sick, but it was nothing compared with the rising nausea of the guilt I felt.

I scanned it quickly, and read it out loud, "'Re: No further need to engage your services. I am writing to you to let you know that you no longer need to attend for work at GLC as the project you were engaged for has been terminated, and therefore your services are no longer required. GLC thanks you for your hard work. As you were engaged as a contractor you are not entitled to a notice period or any redundancy payment but GLC will make a one-off final payment of two weeks' wages as a goodwill gesture.'"

Typical Penny-speak. The insulting letter full of legal terms to basically tell you that you have been chewed up and spat out.

I looked at Liz shiftily. I hadn't been able to bring myself to tell her about my CRB audit, and still couldn't. "It means you've got the sack."

"I thought so. Fuck." Then Liz burst into tears.

"Oh, babe. Please don't."

"You don't get it, do you?" she howled. "I'm on a *working* visa. If I don't get another job within 28 days, my visa won't be valid and I'll have to go home."

I felt like my stomach was full of snakes. I took her in my arms. "I won't let that happen. We'll find you something. In the meantime, why don't you get on the phone to your embassy, or some visa agency somewhere, and check whether there are any loopholes."

She dried her eyes. "Thanks, sweetheart. You are good in a crisis, aren't you? I do love you."

The snakes in my stomach started doing the lambada. I couldn't bring myself to admit I'd been the one who'd got her sacked.

I might have avoided telling Liz some of the less ethical things I'd had to do recently to keep my job, but I had never yet had to lie to her. Today, I felt I had crossed a line. My relationship with her was no longer the honest and pure thing I had put above anything else. I had compromised my integrity for a stupid job. But what else could I do? There was nowhere else in Swinton where I could earn that kind of salary. We needed the money, now more than ever.

I didn't allow myself to realise that if I hadn't been behaving like such a destructive HR cow, Liz would still have her job and we wouldn't be so desperate for my salary. My corruption was complete.

Liz pleaded with her embassy and they managed to buy her some time. She was allowed an extension before she got packed off home on the grounds of being in a relationship with a British citizen. The fact we lived together helped. She managed to wangle an extra two weeks' grace. She had a month and a half before she would be deported.

Liz did apply for jobs, but it was a terrible time to be looking. July was when school-leavers were all competing for the handful of IT jobs needed in mobile phone shops, cafes and bars. Even the youngsters due to go to university out of town seemed to want a couple of month's work during their last summer of freedom at home. It seemed as if there were a dozen applicants going for each vacancy, and half the time Liz didn't even hear back.

PEOPLE PERSON

I couldn't expect my colleagues to understand. Being Swinton born and bred, they had always felt Liz's South African nationality made her a little exotic and removed. They felt that it was only right that local kids took their pick of the available jobs. Someone like Liz was tolerated politely enough, but when it came right down to it, the sense was that she wasn't quite *one of us* and should have perhaps felt grateful that she had ever been able to earn the money that belonged to a British worker by birth right.

Liz very quickly set her sights lower, within two weeks of getting fired from GLC. If no computer jobs were to be hers, perhaps she would be lucky at shop work, pulling pints in one of the pubs, or making sandwiches at the coffee shop and bakery. She was humble and would take anything. She applied to a cleaning company, pest control firm and even in a slight irony, to the church charity committee. It broke my heart to see her put her heart into tailoring her CV, writing covering letters and filling in application forms, and the companies she was counting on to give her work often wouldn't even email her a response. She would wait for weeks with high hopes, until eventually she would have to accept that their HR teams couldn't be bothered to say "no."

With just one more week to go, I had to admit to myself that Liz being out of work had started to cause tension. By the time that sixth week had started, we were having full blown rows. She only had seven days left to save herself and stay in the country. To be with me, for fuck's sake. I didn't want to be a nag, but she looked very much like a waster who had given up even trying. She seemed to be in the house all the time, not contributing anything while I killed myself working long hours for my stupid part-time wage.

It was different now. At first the two of us had looked together for jobs she could go for. Her first and only interview had been over four weeks ago now. She had shone at it, but then been turned down on the basis of the verbal reference from GLC. I had urged her to pursue it, challenge what her last employer had said about her, but Liz's stance was that as it was on the basis of a vaguely negative vibe during a phone call, rather than anything written down she could get hold of and dispute, she thought it simpler to let that one go.

But she just had no plan. No energy to fight back. The weeks ticked by after her only job interview, to my rising panic, but ever since the first tangible rejection, Liz had seemed to give up and resign herself to sitting on the sofa, playing her online games, especially that dreadful one David at work liked, Call of Duty. I heard her muttering into the headphones you wear to play on it, to other lonely individuals playing their games as they had no job or no partner.

I felt so desperately sorry for Liz and I knew that it was all my fault that she had lost her job at GLC. At first, paying her rent and all our bills seemed an appropriate enough sort of penance. But as the weeks dragged on and with the very possible deportation just a week away, I am ashamed to say I started to resent more and more Liz's relaxed approach to her 'kept woman' status. We had to cut back financially, so our social life was non-existent, and every night after a long and horrible day at work, all I had to cheer me up was a miserable boring night in with Liz blanking me, absorbed by her computer game, and some budget meal I could cobble together using the cheapest, least exciting food money could buy.

"You're going to end up being sent back to South Africa," I would plead, but she would just shrug, barely turning her head from the screen, and mutter something about there being nothing more she could do. "Don't you care you won't be with me?" I asked her once. That made her turn to me fully. I still loved her beautiful eyes.

"It's breaking my heart," she said. Then she turned back and lost herself in her game. But I didn't have the emotional resources to feel what I should have felt. My job took everything I had. By the time I got home each night and could concentrate on what was really happening in my life, I felt like a dried-up husk.

I came home one night after seven, to find my lounge full of Liz's friends from the South African pub in Aylham she used to go to all the time before we had met.

They barely looked up from their computer game blaring out of my TV. This irritated me.

"Nice to meet you all," I said sarcastically, picking up a discarded Doritos bag from the floor. The bright orange crumbs from the bottom had spilled onto my beige carpet. I shoved my way through the enormous young men and three lesbians to get close to Liz, who was the one actually playing the game. She steered the controller round me, her eyes not leaving the screen. "When are your friends leaving?" I asked her pointedly.

"...um, not sure..." she said distractedly, as the speakers exploded into gunfire and macho American voices.

"Well, can you ask them to get home, please. I'd like to have a bath and some dinner with you, in peace," I whispered angrily in her ear.

"...I've already eaten, don't worry, love," she said, moving her head from side to side to see round me.

Love? She never calls me that. She calls other women that. Strangers. The word made me realise she had hardly registered who she was talking to. She had retreated into her single life when she had first arrived in England or when she had been living in South Africa. She seemed to be taking comfort from pretending to still be a young singleton with gamer-friends and no responsibilities. What did that make me, then? The woman who would ensure she had a comfortable home and a well-stocked fridge, and never expected her to lift a finger or contribute in any way?

I was not prepared to be Liz's mother.

I stormed into the kitchen to see what we had in for my dinner. Empty beer bottles littered my table, along with two pizza boxes. I found a last slice of pizza and a rogue beer which I helped myself to. Chugging it down in two long swallows helped me calm down a bit. The slice of pizza was cold, the cheese congealing, but it took the edge off my appetite. I yanked open the fridge door to find something more substantial, and gave a grossed-out yell. A stinky pair of trainers sat in the fridge. I threw them on the floor and shouted, "Liz! Why the hell are there trainers in the fridge?"

"...keeping them cool for our basketball tournament later..." her voice came drifting through.

I grabbed the bottle of cava I had saved up for, for our romantic weekend at home together, possibly our last before Liz got on a plane out of my life. If I really had to say goodbye to her, I had planned some low cost lovely couple-y things: I was going to give Liz a massage and run us a big bath, recapture some of the spark we used to have together before we had got so poor and stressed. But why save the cava for that? The way I felt right now, a romantic weekend with Liz was the last thing I wanted. The sight of her made me angry. I popped the cork and raised the bottle directly to my lips. I glugged about half of it without even tasting it.

Liz appeared then. "You OK?" she asked, a frown on her forehead as if she were sure I was fine. "Some of the guys were trying to say you were upset about something."

I rounded on her. "Liz, this isn't like you. Your stoner friends are more sensitive to my needs than you are? Normally I love the way you're so considerate." Resting the neck of the cold bottle to my forehead to cool me down, I realised I was on the verge of tears. "I don't want to live like this," I managed, before my voice broke, waving towards all the empty beer bottles. "Handouts from your mates. You'll be far away from me so soon."

She looked almost as miserable then. "But I don't have anything else," she explained, her voice breaking my heart. "I don't know what else to do. These guys had some information; one of them has been in the same position. He phoned the helpline for me again today, and it is just possible that if I'm out of work but still in a relationship with a Brit, I can get another extension to stay here for a further three months."

I was so tired and stressed from work, I had no resources left to feel glad about this. Looking back, I can't believe I had turned into such a bitch.

She was giving me a weary half-smile. "You are my only hope," she said sadly. We both knew that our relationship was dangling by a thread.

It really shouldn't have been hard to prove to some official that we had a relationship. I loved Liz and I knew she loved me. I was desperate for her to stay with me, and this tiny lifeline should have filled me with elation. Instead, to my shame, the thought of her in my flat for another three months, when I had to keep working so hard to support her and her freeloading friends made me see red. I was just so tired.

"Look, what do you contribute to my life?" I screamed. "I have to pay your rent and your bills – if I lived here on my own I would have slightly more disposable income. I haven't been able to give Amanda anything for the last two months – every spare penny goes on paying back your stupid debt. You're only with me so you don't lose your visa, anyway!" She looked really shocked at that one. I knew I should shut my mouth, but I was so exhausted and virtually hysterical with all the stress. "Living here rent-free means you can stay in the country. I was going to surprise you with this – " I waved the cava bottle at her, "and suggest we spent the weekend in bed. But I can't stand the sight of you right now. You've ruined everything."

PEOPLE PERSON

"Well, then," Liz's voice was scarily calm. I knew I'd gone too far. "If you can ask me what I contribute to your life and all you've got in your mind is money, then you're not the girl I fell in love with. You have changed, Louisa. I've defended you for long enough."

That was a wake-up call. "Defended me? Who to?"

But she didn't answer that, just shook her head slightly with a terrible smile. "That's all I needed to know. I won't bother you anymore."

She disappeared to the lounge. I thought she had returned to playing her game, but shortly afterward I heard the front door slam. When I went through to apologise, everyone had left, including Liz.

I was alone.

Chapter Fifteen

Sunna's face appeared at the door with a ghostly blue paste all over it. She had unbraided her hair which stood out around her head looking like a combination of an afro and a halo. Her slender figure was shrouded in faded pink pyjamas.

"Whassamatter?" she croaked. She had clearly just woken up.

I dragged my suitcase into her hallway. "I'm so sorry about this. Liz and I had a terrible fight about her getting sent back to South Africa and everything, but we've kind of split up, I think, and she left…" I had to pause as my voice was breaking.

"Split up?"

"Yes. I think so." I hung my head. "I've been such a bitch. I don't think she's coming back," I warbled, the tears not far away. "…and I just can't bear to be in that house on my own. Could I possibly stay here for a couple of nights?"

"Course, babe, course." She waved a hand at the pull-out sofa bed I had stayed on once before after a night out. "Make yourself at home. Let me just get this gunk off my face. I was doing a face-pack ready for my date tonight but I must have dozed off." With a click she muted the sound on her big plasma TV. The end of Thelma and Louise was playing. "What time is it anyway?" She peered blearily at the clock made out of an old vinyl record I got her for her birthday. "Geez!

He'll be here in half an hour." She looked at me with the panic of conflicting loyalties.

"Don't mind me, I'll just stay here and watch TV. You go out and have a great time." The words were no sooner out of my mouth than I burst into tears. What was wrong with me? I had never felt so miserable in my life. Liz had left, absolutely everything had turned to shit, and it was all my fault – I had driven her away. I felt like dirt.

Sunna put her arm round me. "I'm going to go and ring him, and cancel," she soothed.

"Oh, no, you don't have to do that…" I sobbed.

"Shhh-hh. I want to. Dates come and go, but friends are forever, right? Let me just go call him and I'll be right back."

I blew my nose and tried to compose myself while Sunna was gone. Feeling embarrassed and in need of comfort food, I jumped up and went to her tiny kitchen. Sunna never cooked so had no need for any more than a kettle, toaster, and microwave. I pulled open the door to her knackered little refrigerator. It didn't contain much in the way of food. Bottles of ready mixed cocktails, including Cosmopolitans and Mojitos. A jar of green olives. A pot of aloe vera face cream and a chillable eye mask. I tried the freezer compartment and found a big bag of ice and a bottle of Grey Goose vodka. Sunna, the homemaker.

She bustled into the kitchen. "It was only Tyrone I was seeing tonight, and it will do him good for me to cancel on *him* at the last minute for a change. Now, my love, if you've been dumped, then there's only one way to get over that."

"Which is?"

"We're going out on the pull."

I blinked at this. Sunna being straight, me being gay, how could we both go out on the pull together successfully?

"We're going to the Candy Bar," she chuckled. "I always wanted to go there. And don't think you're the only person in the world who can turn women's heads, eh."

Sunna. What would I do without you? Sacrificing her date with the beautiful Tyrone, to sit in a lesbian bar with me. I had felt exhausted, but her enthusiasm gave me a tiny lift of energy. Her mad plans were a wonderful distraction from all the pain and self-reproach.

"Now, you, sweetheart, need a makeover," she said, giving me an appraising eye. "You've got an incredible curvy figure and you're not dressing to show it off."

"Translation – I've put on a ton of weight and I'm doing my best to hide it."

Sunna made a noise of scorn a bit like a coffee percolator. "You need to wear colours, and dress like you're happy, like you're in love with life. Then you'll draw people to you."

She marched me upstairs, and despite my protests stripped off my terrible grey hooded top and black tracksuit bottoms, leaving me pimply and wobbly in my underwear. She pulled me in to a bright pink boob tube and a denim mini skirt. "I can't have my bingo wings out!" I squawked. She concealed them brilliantly with a slimming black bolero. We're the same size in shoes, so she forced me to try on some thigh-high boots. Then she tousled my hair, pulled through some sort of spiky Alice band, and slicked a tangerine gloss over my lips.

"Well?" she asked, pushing me in front of the mirror.

I had to admit I looked pretty hot, and it had been a very long time since I had last thought that. I would never have thought to choose such bright colours or show so much skin, but somehow she had brought out my best features and magically reduced my worst. I felt my confidence grow just a little as I stared at the attractive stranger in the mirror.

"I could go for you, myself," Sunna giggled.

She took my hand and lead me down to the leather sofa in the lounge. She turned off Thelma and Louise and set some thumping club music loud on the stereo. Then she disappeared to the kitchen and re-emerged bearing an enormous jug of some cocktail or other with two martini glasses. "Down in one!" she cackled. After the first two drinks, she swiped a metallic turquoise sparkle powder around her eyes and came back from her bedroom in the most incredible white Lycra dress: skin-tight, low and short. Her panther-like muscular body was show-cased to perfection. I was feeling quite trolleyed and pretty much ready for anything. Slipping the bottle of vodka in her handbag for the journey, she led me out to the waiting taxi she'd magicked up, and we disappeared off for a night on the town.

My thoughts were full of my argument with Liz and my sadness that we couldn't be together, but I was just about distracted enough to forget about it for minutes at a time by the time we reached the famous bar. I hadn't been there since I had first come out, when I'd been young and wide-eyed at all the confident gay women in their designer clothes. Back then, I had always been part of a large group of friends and had usually ended up dating one of them. I'd never had the guts to speak to anyone new. "It's packed!" I whispered to her. "We'll have to stand at the bar…and it's three deep – we'll never get served…."

Sunna was incorrigible. She strode around the place as if she owned it, charming some girls into letting us sit at their table and then convincing one of them to go and queue at the bar to get our drinks. She made outrageous eye contact with everyone, flirting and befriending like a pro. You would think she went there every night. I was shyer, and perched on my chair not knowing quite where to put my hands or where to look. Sunna's confidence had swept me in to the bar but by now my excitement was feeling a lot like fear.

"Don't be so nervous!" she whispered to me. "You really look fantastic, you know. Any woman here would be lucky to have you."

"You are nice." Our drinks arrived, and the woman who had got them for us started a conversation with Sunna about holidays, although she seemed more interested in staring down Sunna's barely-there dress. Left alone, I gulped my drink and the room began to spin. After all the vodka in the taxi, I was way over my limit.

Sunna broke away long enough to announce we were all going downstairs to dance. The whole table of eight or nine girls came with us. Sunna was laughing and dispensing anecdotes. I was trying not to fall over.

A woman who'd introduced herself as Sarah grabbed my hand as I almost fell down the stairs. "Steady…" she said, and led me down the rest of the way.

"Thanks," I mouthed, hurrying to keep up with Sunna.

On the dance floor, Sunna was whipping around, dancing with first one woman, then another. She was getting loads of attention. She didn't care though – she never did, and that was the secret of her success. She came to check on me. I was lurking at the edge of the dancefloor, sipping a bottle of beer that Sarah had brought me.

"So – who do you fancy?" Sunna asked me, her eyes shining.

A tricky one. My usual type was long forgotten since I had met Liz. I couldn't help critically comparing anyone else with her, as if she were now my model of perfection. However…pre-Liz, I had usually gone for a handsome, kind butch…like Sarah. "She's nice," I murmured, indicating Sarah with an eyebrow. I felt my face heat up.

Sunna knew who I meant immediately. "I knew it! She hasn't taken her eyes off you," she whispered, "Go on, chat her up."

"Oh, no – I can't – "

"Of course you can! Why not?"

"I'm still so…I don't know, confused. All I can think about is Liz. I haven't been out with anyone else for years. I can't flirt with anyone else. I wouldn't know what to say!"

"Just ask her about herself…" Sunna was not going to let it drop. She was doing a very good impression of a mother bird with a fledgling refusing to leave the nest. "Go on!"

"So Sarah…" I started. She *did* look interested, Sunna had been right there. "What do you do?"

Sarah chuckled. "I don't define myself by my job. In my spare time, I love to take photos."

"I'm an HR Manager," I said without thinking.

"Twenty-four seven?" Sarah grinned.

"Feels like it. I've been focusing on my career recently."

"So what do you enjoy doing if you ever get any free time?"

This conversation was freaking me out. Her words kept repeating themselves in my head as if they were the answers I had been searching for for a very long time. *Define myself by my job…what do you enjoy doing?* I had never asked myself what I enjoyed doing. I do what is needed by the people around me. I do what pays well. And I had defined myself by my job for so long, I had no idea who I was when I wasn't working.

It was embarrassing not to be able to think of a single thing I truly enjoyed. Embarrassing and sad. When had I last been happy?

The photos of little Joseph and Adam were the only thoughts in my head.

"I love children," I slurred, the thought feeling a little like a cartoon lightbulb above my head.

"Me too!" Sarah beamed. "D'you have any of your own?"

"No. Two gorgeous nephews, though."

"Well, that's fantastic. I bet they think the world of you."

"I don't spend as much time with them as I'd like," I continued, more to myself than to anyone else.

"Because of the famous career? That's a shame," Sarah teased. "Bet they'd like to see more of their HR Manager auntie."

Sunna chose that moment to request the DJ play some ridiculous song she'd danced to on a holiday. There were actions and a whole routine for the chorus. She whirled around; getting us all to join in, and

Sarah and I were temporarily separated. Dizzy from dancing, I suddenly felt really sick. Dashing to the loos, I stopped when I saw that the queue to the ladies' was so long that it was out of the door of the communal sink area.

"You don't look so good, sweetheart," the woman in front of me said. "You're ever so pale."

I couldn't reply. I was hot and nauseous. If I opened my mouth, I might hurl where I stood. It was taking all my concentration not to vomit.

Sarah appeared like a knight in shining armour, took one look at me, and muscled her way through the queue. "Coming through, sick girl, excuse us," she bellowed, pulling me behind her by my clammy hand. She wrenched open a cubicle door to reveal two women grappling and kissing. "You can do that outside," she barked. "Look at her," she said, indicating me. As the women were about to protest, I felt my gag reflex give. I shoved past them and spewed my guts into their toilet. They must have gone away because Sarah was there, lifting my hair away from my face and rubbing my back.

I was sick until I was exhausted. I had gone from feeling too hot, to suddenly cold and sweaty. I must have looked absolutely terrible. Breaking away from Sarah, I ran to the sinks and rinsed my face and mouth as best I could. I desperately wanted to clean my teeth.

Sunna appeared. "You OK, babe?"

"Not really. Sorry. I've got to go home."

"Of course, my darling – I'll get us a taxi."

Sarah helped me out of the loos. "You look after yourself," she said. "Drink a pint of water before you go to sleep." Before we left, she slipped her number in my pocket and gave me a wink.

Back at Sunna's, she put me to bed on the sofa. She emptied out her plastic bathroom bin and gave it to me in case I threw up again. When I had assured her I would be fine, she went upstairs to her own bed.

I waited till I was sure she had gone until I let myself cry. What an idiot I was. I hadn't drunk like that in years. Wasn't I supposed to be a grown up, a professional?

Before Liz had left she had given me some home truths, the kind you blurt out when you're past caring how much you hurt the other person. She had said, "Louisa, if you keep chasing money you'll never be happy. Do what you love, do what you do best." Yeah, right. When I do what I do best, people say I'm "too nice" for modern day

PEOPLE PERSON

HR. Louisa the peacemaker. Everybody's friend. Louisa who can see both sides.

Man, I was drunk and miserable. I had only poured the booze down my neck to try and blot out the pain of Liz leaving. But I didn't want to be single. I didn't want to be a drunken young girl who got phone numbers in bars. I wanted to be in a couple. If I was honest, what I wanted was a family.

Chapter Sixteen

Wednesday

I woke at around five in the morning and padded through to Sunna's kitchen in desperate need of water. My head was pounding but I felt strangely focused. A night out had vividly shown me what I didn't want from my life. I climbed back onto the sofa and tried to go back to sleep. There was no sound from upstairs. My mobile rang at seven.

I grabbed the phone, fearing the worst. Death or disaster phones early and late. "Hello?"

It was Eddie. "So sorry to disturb you, Lou. Amanda's sick in bed, temperature through the roof, and your mum's in Gran Canaria. Could you possibly help out with the school run this week? I wouldn't ask but, well – " There was a crash and a howl from one of the boys in the background. "…we're desperate."

I looked at the clock and did a quick calculation. Amanda's house was only ten minutes away, but the school traffic was another story. I was not the sort of person who turned up late for work. But being the sort of person I was hadn't got me very far recently, had it? Oh, sod it. Family come first. "Yes, of course," I told Eddie. "Have you got enough breakfast for me?"

I tiptoed up to Sunna and saw her rueful grin from a mess of pillows and a black satin duvet. "Feeling all right?" were her first words to me.

"Not as bad as I thought I would. I've got to go though."

"Go? Why?"

"My sister needs a hand. I'll head straight into work afterwards."

"Not me," she groaned. "I reckon I've earned a sickie, today." And she flopped back into her bed.

"Sunna! You've got to go in to work!"

"You're such a goody two-shoes! I'm hating my job at the moment. Listen, come round and stay again tonight, if you like, babe. Or any time."

"Thanks, Sunna. I appreciate that."

Sunna's flat was in the slightly nicer road which ran parallel with our slow-running river. A wide and pretty offshoot of the Thames, it carved its way in a North-East to South-West diagonal through the heart of Swinton. Needing to get back across the river at that time in the morning was no joke. We only have a total of two bridges to service the whole town, and budget cuts meant the promised repairs and widening of one bridge had been indefinitely postponed, after the bridge itself had been cordoned off with traffic cones and plastic ribbon. In my rust-bucket car, praying I wasn't still over the limit, I crawled to the bridge that was still in action, and queued with the commuters who were making their way to the lucrative jobs of London.

As I let myself in to my sister's flat, the smoke alarm was going off. I crashed through the lounge, which seemed to be carpeted with Lego and Mini Racers, to the kitchen and snatched the bits of charcoal that had presumably been toast from under the grill.

Eddie and the boys were nowhere to be seen. I got the mop out of the utility cupboard and used the long handle to poke frantically at the shrill alarm until I succeeded in turning the damn thing off. Then I opened the back door to let the smoke out.

I heard thundering on the stairs, and Joseph and Adam appeared. Joseph was naked apart from his nappy while Adam was in most of his school uniform except he had his tie round his head and he was making the classic Cowboys and Indians noise, flapping his hand over his mouth to make the 'wah-wah-wah' sound. Eddie appeared in his shirt and underpants and chased Adam with his socks trying to get them on his feet through a mixture of telling off and pleading.

PEOPLE PERSON

"Hi, Lou, thanks so much for coming," Eddie puffed, snatching the knife out of Joseph's hands as he passed with the sock. "Smells like the toast's a goner." He looked grimly at the kitchen clock. "I should have been in Gravesend five minutes ago."

"You go," I said. "I'll take over here."

"Are you sure?" His face was a picture of gratitude.

"Yes, go!"

Bless Eddie. He and Manda worked so hard. Maybe the boys would appreciate it one day.

"Now you two," I said sternly to my little charges. "Auntie Lou's in charge this morning, so no nonsense, OK?" Joseph looked up at me with enormous horrified eyes while Adam fell about laughing. I got them sat at the table and brought their colouring books and pens from the big plastic boxes in the lounge. "Competition time, boys. Who can colour me the most beautiful picture to stick on my fridge? Careful you don't go over the lines."

Silence descended as Adam carefully coloured a picture of a clown all in black, and Joseph scribbled all over a tableau of the tortoise and the hare. While they were busy, I ransacked the cupboards and got a healthy family breakfast underway. Porridge, fruit juice, and boiled eggs with toast soldiers. The boys wolfed down everything as soon as it was ready. Then I sat them in front of the early morning cartoons while I took a tray up to their mother.

Amanda looked terrible. She was white with sunken, sallow hollows around her eyes, and her hair was stuck to her damp forehead.

"Thanks so much for the food, but I can't manage it at the moment." She couldn't lift her head off the pillow and she could only speak in a croaky whisper, "If you leave it there I might try it later." I held the glass of orange juice so she could raise her head slightly and take a sip.

"Are you sure you're going to be all right?"

"I'll be fine," she smiled. "You need to get to that important job of yours. Thank you so much for driving the boys. You know where you're going?"

I nodded. I'd done the school run once before when Eddie was having his appendix out.

I gave her a kiss on her damp hair. "You'll be all right, sis. I'll call you at lunchtime." If I get a lunch break, I thought, but I'd worry about that later.

I fitted the booster seats into my old banger and joined the gridlock, first to Adam's school. We charged through the gates at ten to nine, and grabbing his packed lunch and book bag, Adam ran into the playground to join his friends without a single look back at me.

Holding Joseph in my arms, I paused by the school gates to catch my breath. I heard a voice I vaguely recognised say, "Louisa Cannes? Is that you?"

I turned to see Rachel Wigmore, a former classmate, dropping off two boisterous little girls from her enormous people carrier. "I haven't seen you in ten years! Is this your little boy?"

"Oh, no!" I laughed. "This is my nephew. I don't have any of my own."

"Oh, sorry." She flushed and looked a little awkward.

"Don't be!" I realised I was blushing too, and started to gabble, "I haven't got round to the whole baby thing, yet. Too busy working."

"That's right. I thought I heard from Mum you had an amazing career these days," she smiled. "Good for you."

"Thanks." I wish it felt as good as everyone else thought it was. "What are you up to, yourself?"

"Oh, nothing as exciting as you. The girls keep me busy and I run a couple of aqua-aerobics classes at the gym. You should come! It's a laugh, not too strenuous."

"Maybe I will." Her life sounded so relaxing. "Well, I'd better get Joseph round to nursery."

"Is it Little Angels you take him to?"

I nodded.

She looked at her watch. "It's nearly nine, and you know that they fine you if you're late."

Argh. "Thanks – I'd better run – "

Chapter Seventeen

Slamming the car door, I revved up and nosed my way out of the ridiculous school traffic. How did I not know such a basic premise about childcare? Just when I was looking longingly at the life of a full-time mum, I find out I'm not qualified. I don't know the first thing about it. How much are these nursery fines, anyway? I doubted I even had five pounds in cash on me.

We crawled along and Joseph started grizzling. "It's OK, poppet, nearly there." To distract us both, I put on the radio, and started pressing buttons to try and find something more child-friendly that my usual classic rock. More inadequacy on my part. Manda's car was stuffed full of CDs of nursery rhymes and stories.

Joseph was really bawling. I turned round to look at him and was greeted by horns blaring. Blimey, had I swerved the steering wheel as I turned round? How do mothers manage all this?

I focused on the road and pulled over into a parking space as soon as I could. I phoned Jason. He had returned to work now after his injuries had become less visible. He was almost back to his cheerful self.

He answered with his usual, "Yo, boss." My mobile announces my number on his work phone.

"Hi, mate, I'm running late this morning." Joseph chose that moment to give out his most anguished howl so far.

Jason's laughter could be heard down the crackly line. "Boss, what are you doing to that poor kid?"

"Long story. Please could you have a look in my Outlook Calendar? I don't think I've got any meetings this morning, from memory, but I just wanted to be sure."

There was a short pause while he looked. "Nope. You're clear all day. A few things have happened this morning but it's all stuff I can handle – I'll update you when you arrive."

"You're a star. Thanks a million."

Now I had work off my mind, I could focus properly on Joseph's woes. Sniffing the air, I thought I might have figured out the source of his discomfort. His nappy needed changing. I rifled through the bag of equipment Eddie had left me with. I located a clean nappy and baby wipes, but where was I supposed to lie Joseph out to change him? I had only ever had a go at changing his nappy when he was lying down on Manda's second-hand baby changing mat on the floor of her lounge.

I supposed I was going to have to make enough space in the back of my car. Unbuckling the booster seat Adam had vacated, I had two clear seats next to Joseph. Grabbing my picnic blanket from the boot, I spread it out in an attempt to protect my upholstery from baby poo. Pinning Joseph down to it, I grimly started changing his nappy.

Joseph found the experience enchanting and stopped crying immediately. He laughed and giggled, trying to wiggle away, and almost disappeared off the edge of the car seat into the foot well beneath.

"Stay still, my darling," I muttered, before he decided this was a brilliant new game.

Dear God, there was dark green baby poo absolutely everywhere. I used half a pack of baby wipes cleaning him up, and then needed the other half for my hands, arms, back of car seat and somehow my face where I'd wiped my eyes. Finally I'd got him happily swaddled in a beautiful white nappy covered with pictures of happy, well-fed babies.

"Right, mate, back in the car seat and off we go to nursery – about an hour late."

My phone rang again just as I was setting off. I parked at a crazy angle and grabbed my phone. "What?" I snapped.

It was Eddie. "Look, Lou, sorry to disturb you…."

"I'm just taking Joseph to nursery – what's up? You sound terrible."

His voice broke and I felt as if the bottom had dropped out of my stomach. "It's Manda. She got much worse and called herself an ambulance. She's in St Peter's – I'm there now."

"No!" St Peter's was our nearest hospital in neighbouring Dene. Joseph was starting to fuss and wiggle on the back seat. I reached out to his tummy and rubbed it to keep him occupied.

"They don't know what she's got so they're running loads of tests. But she's very weak and they won't let me see her at the moment." He started properly crying then. It was terrifying to hear macho Eddie breaking down in painful, choking sobs.

"I'll be right there. I'll drop Joseph first so you won't have to worry about him till later, and then I'll come and wait with you."

"Thanks, Lou."

Work would have to wait. My big sister had always seemed invincible. I couldn't bear to think of her all alone and vulnerable in a hospital bed.

I got Joseph to Little Angels and before the stern nursery lady could tell me off for being so late, I explained that his mum had been taken into hospital. My voice was cracking and my lips were trembling as I told her the little I knew. She melted and asked if there was anything they could do.

"Nothing at the moment. I'll do my best to pick him up on time at the end of the day." She looked as if she was reluctantly going to have to warn me about fines or something if I was late again, so I left my business card with all my numbers on it and fled. I jumped in my car and set off again for the hospital, becoming the world's most aggressive driver as I hooted and swore my way back through the gridlock.

On the way, on a stretch of road that might as well have been a car park for all the progress we were making, I used the time to phone Jason again. "Bad news, I'm afraid – my sister's really ill and I'm not sure I'll be able to make it in at all today. Will you guys be all right?"

"I'm fine, but –" Jason sounded like he was closing my office door. He was whispering when he came back on the line. "Penelope got wind that you're not here and she threw a fit. She's demanding you get into her office the second you arrive."

"Oh, for F –" I couldn't believe this. What could be so important that she needed me there and then? "Is she around now, to speak to?"

"No, she's in with the Board. I'll put you through to Mike."

Chapter Eighteen

I crawled through the traffic up Apple Hill. I would inch forward then stop, then have to do another hill start and my right leg was cramping from all the breaking and revving. I glanced back at where Joseph had been lying and realised I missed having him with me already.

Mike came on the line. He was furious. "What were you thinking, Louise?"

"What do you mean?" I was pretty angry myself. "Everyone has a family emergency from time to time, it's just life. My sister's in hosp –
"

"I'm talking about the five projects you didn't tell me about. The Senior Management Team Minutes are full of it. I'm sending you them."

I took my phone away from my face to receive the email. My hands were shaking, I was so full of rage. I scrolled quickly down the minutes and saw all the formal language which basically showed Penny slating Mike and then him blaming me for not showing him the papers in advance of presenting them to the Board. Had we been at the same meeting? He had been fine at the time, and I had even split up the projects and showed him one at each supervision meeting over five months so he would have time to consider and agree each one. I shoved the phone back on my ear, struggling to keep from shouting at him.

"Mike, I can see the minutes where you're giving the impression that I didn't share these projects with you…."

"The point is, you should have brought them to the Senior Management Team meeting before the Board meeting."

"Oh! Well, sorry, but you didn't tell me that. You needed to make that clear when I explained each one to you in our one-to-ones! Do you remember me saying I wanted to bring in these five projects, that's why they needed Board approval?"

"Look, Louise," Mike raised his voice over mine. "You've made me look a laughing stock at Senior Management Team and with the Board. This is very serious indeed."

There was only one explanation for a reaction like this. He must have got a bollocking from Penny.

"Look, Mike, I don't agree with you but I haven't got time to discuss it now. My sister's really ill in hospital, and I never take time off. I've been really flexible with GLC – working late and weekends as you know, even working for a part-time wage to help out! But this time I need you and Penelope to be flexible and help me out, and I hope you can understand that."

I disconnected and threw the phone into the back seat before Mike had a chance to respond. To be honest, I was past caring what he said. If my sister needed me to sit beside her hospital bed, then that's where I'd be, job or no job.

I finally made it to St Peter's. I found Eddie in some horrible waiting area, his huge muscular frame taking up two of the orange plastic folding seats. For a crazy moment, I looked at my seat as I flapped it down, and it reminded me of a cinema, the way the seats fold down. I remembered being on a double-date with Eddie and Manda, me and my then girlfriend. We had been young then, and life had been simple. I had made my sister laugh so hard with my impression of Mrs. Doubtfire, she had shot half-chewed popcorn out of her mouth and sprayed the prim couple in the row in front of us.

I put my arm round as much of Eddie's hulking shoulders as I could reach. "How you doing, big fella."

"Not good." He was welling up already. "I need to be strong for Manda and our boys." He blew his nose like he had a trombone in his handkerchief.

I didn't know what to say but I needed positivity as much as he did. What do people say to each other when this kind of thing happens on a soap or in a film? "She's a fighter. She'll pull through." I was making this stuff up. How the hell did I know whether Manda was going to live or die in that hospital bed? But comforting Eddie somehow pushed away my own fear. If I let myself think about how I was actually feeling, I'd have let go and started bawling the place down.

"Has anyone spoken to Mum?" I asked him.

"No," he said, guiltily. "There didn't seem to be time on the way here, and now I can't use my phone inside the hospital, but I didn't want to leave in case they came out with some news and I wasn't here…"

"Don't worry, I understand. Well, there's two of us here now, so I'll go outside and give her a ring. Mum left me the number of her hotel, even if her mobile's switched off. Just promise me if there's any news on Manda, you'll come out and tell me."

I tried my mum's mobile but she had it switched off as she usually did on holiday, since she had found out how much it cost to get connected or even receive a text in Gran Canaria. She's been going there ever since my dad died – a gentleman friend of hers pays for her flight and hotel room so she can join him out there. It's an arrangement I don't want to know too much about, but she always comes back tanned and happy so I'm glad. I hated to ruin her holiday with this but she needed to know about Manda.

I phoned her hotel and it was answered in gabbled Spanish. I said, "Hola, Señor, do you speak English?"

The gruff voice said, "Ye-es, Madam."

I slowed down so that each word was separately enunciated, "Please could I leave a message for Mrs. Cannes."

"Room Seex-ty Huan?"

"Yes, probably. Is she there now?"

"No, no, beach, beach."

"Please ask her to call her daughter on this number."

"Her doctor?"

"Christ. No, her daughter, her bambina. Just tell her to phone this number, please."

"Si, si, Señora. Adios, bye bye bye."

"Adios," I replied, feeling a bit like I was in a Western, my grim sense of humour feeling like a protective shield from the horrible world.

I trooped back inside, and scraping together the coins I had on me, bought two coffees and a chunky Kit Kat. Locating Eddie, we sat and shared the chocolate in silence. After the hour hand on my watch had crawled past two different numbers, we finally saw a doctor. He looked about twelve and was very posh.

"We've isolated the problem, Mr. Smith," he said to Eddie. "Your wife has viral meningitis."

"How serious is it?" Eddie asked.

"It's a very serious condition, I'm afraid." The boy-doctor was hushed and professional. "Not common at all. I understand that Mrs. Smith was very run down."

"She works really hard caring for her sick son," I explained. "But I had no idea…"

"Unfortunately we have seen that a few times recently," the doctor seemed to think this explanation made Manda's frightening condition seem logical, while I was feeling even worse about it, if that were possible. "Carers behave in very selfless ways and seem to ignore their own health. The next few hours will be critical, but we're doing all we can. Rest assured, Mrs. Smith is in the best place. The team are giving her the best care."

"But is she going to be all right?" I squeaked.

Dr. Junior gave me a tired smile much older than his years. "We're doing all we can. I'm afraid you won't be able to see your sister for some time yet. We'll call you the minute there's any change, so I recommend both of you go home and get some rest."

Yeah, right. Why do they always say that in hospitals? As if either of us was going anywhere. Eddie was resigned to sitting for as long as it took in the waiting area, and I was only going to leave that hospital for long enough to go and collect the boys from nursery, give them to the next-door-neighbour friends of Manda's when they got in from work, and get them settled for the night there. I wished I had Manda to ask what they would need. Pyjamas? Toothbrushes?

Then I doubled back to the hospital to sit and wait.

As I made my way from the hospital car park, my phone chirruped into life. I stabbed at it and slammed it against my face, "Mum?"

PEOPLE PERSON

"No, Louisa, it's Penelope," a chilly voice said. "Where on *earth* are you?"

Chapter Nineteen

Christ, Penny on my phone! This was all I needed right now. I had my hand to my forehead, trying not to scream at her or cry. "I'm in the hospital, Penelope. My sister's got meningitis and she was rushed here. I had to ferry her kids around. Didn't Mike tell you?"

A pause.

"Yes...he said you had a 'family emergency.'" Her tone was suspicious.

"Exactly." *So why the hell are you phoning me?*

"I just wanted to make sure you remembered the stipulations of the policy." Penny gave a little sigh, as if I were a difficult child. "Special leave – "

"Uh, I know the policy, Penelope," I cut in, trying my hardest not to yell at her. "Three days' paid leave for a sudden family emergency – "

"*Up to* three days," she spat. "At the discretion of the Director of Human Resources. And the three days are not to carry out care, they are to make arrangements for a more appropriate person to do the caring, so that you can get back to work, where you are needed."

"Who would be more appropriate to take my nephews to school?" I gasped, in spite of my resolution not to argue with this emotionless woman.

"Someone who isn't employed by GLC." Penelope allowed herself a small titter. Personnel humour.

"And I need to be with my brother-in-law, now, Penelope. His wife has a life-threatening illness..." my voice cracked. "And there's no way I'm leaving him on his own."

"It really isn't my concern *who* takes over the responsibility for you, Louisa, as long as *you* are back at work, bright and early, tomorrow morning."

This time, my voice was steady. A deadly calm had crept into me. "Penelope, I don't care how you account for it, but I need a few days off, here."

"But your request for emergency leave has not been agreed by the Director of HR. I have assessed the facts of the case as you have presented them to me, and I do not consider it necessary for you to have any further time off. Today should have been sufficient, had you organised yourself correctly."

"Penny, I'm going to say this just one more time. I will not be in tomorrow morning."

"Then you will be absent without leave, which as you know is a disciplinary matter. Four days of unauthorised absence and your contract of employment will be terminated."

I took a deep breath. Normally I would have been on the verge of tears by now, but the image of Amanda was giving me a steely calm. "You don't need to sack me over this, Penny."

She gave a tiny laugh of triumph. She believed she had won. "Well, I do hope not, Louisa."

I had a smile on my face when I said, "Because I'm resigning."

And I slapped my phone off and stomped back into the hospital to be with my family when they needed me.

Chapter Twenty

My mum got in touch and was on the first flight home from Spain. She said to me when I gave her the bad news, "When your father died, I thought my heart would break. But that would be nothing compared with losing Amanda. I'm not burying one of my baby girls."

I felt as if all the air had been squeezed out of my lungs. "She'll be all right, Mum," I said, sounding much braver than I felt.

By the time my mum arrived at the hospital, it was four in the morning. Eddie and I were asleep, slumped in the plastic chairs in the waiting room. My mouth was dry and my head was thumping.

Mum was wild eyed with fear for Manda. "How is she?" she whispered.

"Still no news," I croaked. I stood up gingerly, and almost fell over on my rubbery legs. Every bit of me felt numb. Sleeping bolt upright in a fold-down seat had taken its toll.

Eddie stirred and said "help" weakly.

There were still patients and visitors arriving despite the time. They spoke in hushed tones with expressions of fear and pain. I couldn't imagine working in a hospital. The staff that appeared to give advice and reassurance seemed tireless. I vowed to leave a huge donation in their air ambulance appeal box next time I had cash on me.

My mum had a handbag full of Spanish chocolate bars and little packaged croissants. I ate one gratefully and wandered off to find a bottle of water. The shop was closed but there was a vending machine. In the faffing around finding someone with change, I almost missed our twelve year old doctor passing by. He seemed to be looking for me and hadn't recognised Eddie, snoring next to Mum.

I pounced on the doctor, "How's Amanda?"

He looked as exhausted as me, but his face creased into a kind smile. "She's on the mend; she responded to the treatment in the best way possible, and she will not need to be moved into the intensive care unit. We will need to keep her with us for some time yet, but you can visit her now, if you'd like to."

"Yes, please!" I could have kissed him. "Let me get my family."

My mum almost screamed when she saw Manda. I thought she might faint; she sort of sagged on her knees, but then rushed over to her bed. Eddie ambled over, sobbing. He was such a sad sight – a big bear of a man, all shoulders and chest, weeping without restraint.

"Sorry to scare you," were Amanda's first words to us. Her hair was all stuck up around her head and some was clinging to her cheeks, just like when she was little and had a temperature.

"How are you feeling?" I asked her in a choking sort of sob.

"Like I've been run over by a truck," she smiled. "But I've been assured I'm not going to die. The night staff have been amazing. I'll see a specialist in the morning and he'll decide how long I've got to stay in for."

My mum had her in her arms, cradled as she sat on the bed, and kissed her forehead every now and then as if she couldn't believe Amanda was real.

My big sister. If I had lost her, there would have been no one to remember our childhood with. No one who knew about the language we made up on family holidays. No one who remembered the way our dad used to smuggle us chocolate when we were in trouble with Mum and sent to our shared bedroom. How could I have wasted so many hours at work and spent so little of my adult life with her?

I gave Manda's hand a final squeeze, "You look after yourself."

We agreed it was sensible for not all of us to stay at the hospital. The boys needed rested guardians to ferry them around. So Mum and I said we'd go home and leave Eddie with Amanda. I don't think we could have dragged him out of that room. He prepared to stay for what was left of the night. One of the nurses took pity on him and brought him a sort of fold-out camp bed to go on the floor beside Manda's bed. I gave him my bottle of water.

I drove my mum to hers, staggering gratefully into her house just as the sun was coming up. Half six. I had a shower and got straight into the spare bed, my hair all wet, too exhausted to stand. With a pang I realised that with no Liz in my flat, there had been no one to wait up for me, no one to worry. Would anyone have sobbed the way Eddie had, if it had been me who had become ill? Apart from my mum, I couldn't think of anyone who cared about me anymore. I'd fucked everything up with Liz. I had behaved so badly at work and alienated so many people I'd been close to; I didn't seem to have any love left in my life. It was a sad thought and it made me feel desperate and alone, so I pushed it away and forced myself to sleep.

I woke briefly at nine and phoned Jason.

"Sorry, mate, I won't be back today," I told him. "I was up all night."

"How's your sister?"

"It was touch and go, but she's going to be fine. I'll get some sleep now and see you tomorrow."

"Did Penny catch up with you?"

"Oh, yes..." I had forgotten about that bit. Not the best of conversations to have to have with Jason. I didn't want to worry him with my petulant resignation. In the literal cold light of day, being out of work sounded rash at best. Still, even if Penelope had taken me seriously, I had my three months' notice period to find something else. "All sorted, don't worry," I lied.

Next I called Mike. He was much kinder than Penelope had been. Genuinely glad to hear that Amanda was going to pull through, and happy to agree a few days' annual leave as long as all my meetings could be rearranged. From his tone of voice, I had a funny feeling Penelope had passed on the information to him about my hysterical resignation threat and he was not mentioning it. He was fine with the thought that Jason was temporarily in charge, and decided he was going to go round to my office and give Jason some support, a kind of pep talk. I got off the phone strangely irked by this. I had worked for Mike come rain or shine, dealt with work catastrophes, had to try my best and guess how exactly to deal with some incredibly difficult situations, but one thing I had never had was managerial support from Mike. He'd never once come to my office when I'd been there to give *me* a pep talk. But I put it out of my mind, angrily telling myself, "you need work to be sorted, you need someone to hold the fort while you take some time out, and it is all taken care of by Jason and Mike between them, so what's your problem?" I ignored the slithering in my stomach which told me that nothing would be the same.

Chapter Twenty-One

Thursday

My mum was resting. She has to sleep until she wakes up, if you see what I mean. An alarm clock or even a careless curtain opening in her room can bring on a migraine that lasts all week.

The shrine to my dad was still in her lounge. She's got an assortment of framed photos of him arranged on top of a dresser, with fresh flowers and two lit candles, always. It's a bit macabre for me. She visits his grave every morning except for when she's away on one of her holidays with her new boyfriend. Figure that one out.

I sat down to wait in her immaculate lounge. She never worked, so she always did have plenty of time for stuff like hoovering and dusting – the things I never do. I probably *do* have the time to do housework, but I just don't. I can't be bothered to do more than the bare minimum. If the place is hygienic, who cares? Life's too short for flower arranging and cushion plumping, as far as I am concerned.

This was the house I grew up in, every inch of it steeped in childhood memories. There was still a chunk missing from the banisters where Manda and I had tied it up with a load of old bicycle chains for Halloween, and come clanking down the stairs dressed as Jacob Marley's ghost (her) and Scrooge (me). Mum's pride and joy, the little upright piano in the very corner of the lounge by the window, had a few ugly flecks of deep blue ink I had managed to shake onto it when using my colouring set nearby. Her chintzy three-piece suite had a few similar flecks, and I vividly remembered her trying every kind of upholstery cleaner on the dots I had inadvertently left there, but nothing would make them budge. I must have been about seven or eight. Running my bare foot over her enormous peach coloured Chinese rug, I reflected that it never would lie flat; the edges always curled up slightly, and that was testimony to the numerous occasions she would roll it back out of our way so that Manda and I could play our boisterous games on the carpet without ruining the rug. We would sit in a giant cardboard box together and make believe it was a pirate ship, and when Dad got home, he would always make one of us walk the plank into the "shark infested" kitchen nearby, till we were breathless with excited laughter.

My mum emerged eventually, her blonde hair swept up into an elegant chignon, her unmade-up face somehow radiant and refined. She had the bone structure of a Russian countess and the complexion of a teenage milkmaid. She was a looker. She looked better, just woken up and on the verge of her sixtieth birthday, than I've ever looked after hours of primping.

My sister takes after my mother, naturally.

Mum swept into the kitchen to put on a pot of coffee. I toddled in her wake.

We sat at her imported butcher block table. Dad's last anniversary gift to her. As her milk frother shuddered and spat, I filled her in on my news.

"Liz has left. She's going back to Johannesburg. We've split up."

Mum reached out and gave my cheek a little stroke with one of her impeccably manicured fingers. "Oh, poppet, I'm sorry. I know you were keen on her."

I felt the tears welling up. "She was the one," I managed, in a squeaky voice.

"What happened? Is there any chance she'll come back?" Mum wanted to know.

"It was all my fault."

She gave me a smile full of experience. "That's unlikely. It takes two to mess up a relationship."

"Well, it was hardly a relationship. I was at work all the time, and then when she lost her job, I felt so resentful that I had to pay her rent and everything."

"I'm sure your father felt like that sometimes."

That stopped me short. I'd never thought about Dad being anything but thrilled about providing for his princess. "But you two were different."

"Why?" Mum asked.

"…well, because he was a…"

"What?" She was smiling again. She knew she had me. She knew I had been about to say, Dad was a man, and so things were different. How annoying – I was usually the one getting aerated about gender equality.

Mum tried a different tack, "Whose idea was it for Liz to move out?"

"Hers. She said she didn't want to be a burden any more. No, wait. It was me who said she was a burden." Mum's eyes were suddenly dark with reproach. I saw reflected in them the extent of my crime. I should never have made my girlfriend feel unwelcome. What a bitch! But I had been so tired and stressed. "If I hadn't been working so many hours I would have been more tolerant."

"What's a job, really?" Mum asked. "I know I'm no expert, but I thought the point was it was supposed to give you money to enjoy the rest of your life, not become the focus of it. Would you rather have a career than a partner?"

"Well, at the moment I don't have either!" I exploded, storming over to the fridge. Just like my dad. Short-tempered and a glutton. I ripped open the door and searched in vain for junk food. All I saw were M&S superfood salads and designer mineral water. Mum's honey and cream face pack looked the most appetising. "Liz told me to do what I'm good at, do what I enjoy."

"Well, that's sound advice," Mum soothed.

I gave up searching her fridge. "Why don't I take us out for breakfast, Mum. My treat."

ALEX SPEAR

Chapter Twenty-Two

Manda was weak and needed regular blood tests, but the hospital did let her go home on Monday. I had only really needed a couple of working days off, but not going into GLC on all the days I wasn't paid for, I mean the Friday, Saturday and Sunday, had really been a wake-up call for me. I couldn't believe how much better I felt for spending some proper quality time with the people I cared about. I decided then and there that helping out at Manda's house and spending time with her would be the focus of my free time.

By Tuesday, having assured myself that Manda was fine and Mum was going to spend the day with her, I went back to work. My hasty resignation was forgotten. I felt uneasy, humiliated even, but I did need the money.

You see, Penelope had phoned me back on my mobile towards the end of breakfast with my mum on the Thursday before. I had just got a rough plan in my head of how I would manage by setting up my own consultancy and scouring London for projects I could charge for. Discussing it with Mum, I had actually been feeling quite relieved not to be working at GLC anymore. But suddenly, there was Penny, claiming me like her slave once again. On the phone, barely audible over the breakfast cafe hubbub, she had murmured some words which sounded almost like a prayer.

"Beg pardon?"

As she repeated it I realised she was quoting case law. The woman was bonkers! She said she understood I'd been under a lot of pressure when I'd threatened to resign, and therefore in line with the case law she was muttering about, she wanted to give me the chance to withdraw my notice.

I was surprised, but very suspicious. I said, "Yes, please, I'd like to carry on working at GLC if it's possible, thank you. I appreciate that."

I don't know whether it was the relief of realising that I had the guts to leave GLC if I wanted to, or whether it was seeing my family so rocked by a real problem that put work into some sort of perspective, but whatever it was, I was feeling a little more assertive. I resolved to take charge of my career. Maybe I had to stick it out in this horrible role at GLC, but I could increase the amount of experience I was getting of the things that interested me, couldn't I? Then the next time I was looking for a job, I would have the right stuff on my CV to get into an area I really enjoyed.

Perhaps I was naive, or perhaps my natural optimism meant I couldn't imagine the revenge Penelope was capable of. Hadn't I learnt anything? A reasonable request from Sam had been enough to incite Penny's evil. She interpreted any of her underlings asserting their own opinion as insubordination which could not be allowed to go unpunished. She had even ensured that Sam would not be able to work in HR again, due to the "evidence" I had manufactured and the damning reference Penelope ensured she would be given, wherever she worked in future. I don't know why I was so trusting and stupid, not to imagine that Penny was keeping me close just so that she could build a similar case against me, to destroy me utterly. In any case, I carried on at work, blissfully unaware of the trap being set for me.

Do what you're good at, I thought. Do what you enjoy. Rather than apologising for the kind of person I am, or pretending to be something I am not, I resolved to embrace my sense of fair play as a strength.

I planned to put my skills in seeing both sides of an argument to good use. Maybe I was ashamed of the cut-throat approach of modern-day HR, but one thing that I knew that old-fashioned personnel could still help with was resolving the disputes of people who have to work together every day. I knew there was a grievance between two members of the call centre, and so to get some experience of soothing the ruffled feathers, I volunteered to mediate between the two who were angry with each other.

I knew a little bit about the staff involved. The aggrieved, David, took out a grievance against one of his colleagues, seemingly at random, approximately once every six months. He seemed very easily upset by others. Some would say he was a grumpy old man who didn't really want to spend time with anyone but needed the money so had to find a way to jog along with his long-suffering colleagues. Heather, the unfortunate member of his team who was on the receiving end of his latest grievance, hadn't worked with us long and was still learning the ropes. I wondered whether she found it hard to put him in his place.

David was interrupting me even while I was explaining the structure of the meeting. It was the first mediation meeting I had chaired and I was nervous but determined to do a good job. I was just explaining to David that after he had gone through all of his gripes, Heather would have a chance to respond if she wanted, then we would go through all her complaints. David interrupted me to say, "And there's no need for this to be adversarial, Heather. I'll explain the word to you both. Adversarial means…."

"We're familiar with the word, David," I spat, raising my voice over his. Patronising git. He had adopted the pose of a barrister: one hand holding his lapel, the other hand in an aggressive finger-pointing style to emphasise every word. Opposite him sat tough yet self-effacing Heather, who had her skinny legs wrapped around one another, gripped so tightly that the muscles were crushed, and her hands bound together on the desk in front of her in an attitude of supplication or prayer.

You would have thought that David was Heather's manager from the way he spoke to her, but this just wasn't the case. They were colleagues on the same level, and if anything, David was probably the one in the wrong. His grievance had mysteriously come about after he had been caught out and embarrassed at work. He had forgotten to come in to work for a late shift, and Heather had ended up hanging around past the end of her shift waiting for him to arrive so she could go. They shared a desk and had to make sure that between them their phone wasn't left without cover. In the end Heather had been waiting for so long that she had had to phone David at home, to tell him to get dressed, stop playing Call of Duty and come on shift because he had clearly forgotten. Before David had managed to hot-foot it into work, their manager had discovered him missing and got the truth out of

Heather. She had shielded David for as long as she could, but couldn't magic him to the office, and he had got into trouble for his unreliability. Served him right, pompous know-it-all, his colleagues had thought. If he had accepted the telling off with good grace, he might have actually won some respect as being human. Instead, in his uptight way, David had then taken umbrage at a minor remark of Heather's on another shift they were working together, and was now using the grievance policy against her. The cynical might say he wanted revenge for being embarrassed, and a timid colleague was easier to take it out on than the manager.

Heather tried to say three times, "David, it might just be your manner..." before he cut her off. In the end I had to jump in. Mindful that he thought there was bias against him, I just raised a hand and said gently, "David, let Heather make this point and then we'll come back to yours."

He didn't like it but he shut up for a second. Heather didn't need asking twice. She sat bolt upright in the chair and let rip. "David, you put me down, you constantly mention your degree, I haven't got a degree – I didn't finish school – but I know what I'm talking about. I can do my job. You're not my manager, and I'm asking you to speak to me like we're equals, not always like I'm your...your..." She struggled for the word.

David tried to help. "Subordinate? I'll explain the word to you both. Subordinate means...."

"I know what it means!" she exploded with some exasperated laughter.

Ah. I pricked up my ears. Laughter was good. Looking at David, he actually seemed to have a slightly abashed grin. Could some self-awareness be dawning on the man? Surely not some humility?

"What would you like to be different, David?" I asked.

He pondered, and then said in a small voice, "Well, I have been doing this job for six years now. It *would* be nice if the newbies would listen to me. I *have* seen it all before."

I went into solution mode. "Well, David, I think rather than saying that to Heather, you would best off saying that to your manager, don't you think? You could help with the induction and on-the-job training of the "newbies." That way they could hear from you, first-hand, what works and what doesn't."

PEOPLE PERSON

"Yes! Yes! I could!" His eyes were shining. "I have lots of ideas for a better initial training programme than we use at the moment...." Heather was actually listening to his plans with something approaching respect. I knew that it would take further work to help them rebuild their relationship, but I could see that the dialogue was open again. Both the angry combatants felt listened to and understood, so that they could relax and work together as a team. And I had created that.

So, my job was starting to feel a little more rewarding. Without any help from Mike, the worst line manager I could have had, I was enriching the experience I was getting, and increasing the amount of time each week that I was doing stuff I enjoyed. I was still working a six day week for four days of pay, but for the first time in a long while, I felt as if I had a little bit of a plan. I was making money, but I was not just marking time. There was light at the end of the tunnel.

I could do this for a bit longer, I thought. I visited Manda and helped out with the boys. I went to work and made a conscious effort to grab opportunities that gave me personal satisfaction. Where possible, I delegated or ignored the tasks that didn't play to my strengths.

For the first time in a long time, my little life felt contented enough.

But Penny, it seemed, had other ideas.

Chapter Twenty-Three

One piece of work I couldn't put off any longer was to meet the poor night workers and tell them that from April, they would be docked the pay they had received for their break times. It was one of the classic HR issues I had really decided I didn't want to do any more, but there was no way I was going to delegate such an unpopular decision. I was going to face up to these people and give them the respect of a personal discussion. If Mike had had his way, he recommended just sending a mass email to them all, hoping no doubt that because they worked at night and slept all day, the affected staff would never be in the building when we were.

What a cowardly approach. The least we could do was speak to them and give them a human face to ask questions of. Let them shout, let them vent.

I'd stayed up all night to tell the night workers that their breaks were now unpaid. They had been understandably angry with me. I held a meeting of about 45 of them with their union reps, and they had had lots of questions for me as well as general complaints. While I certainly didn't enjoy their grilling, I forced myself to be nice in response. I felt for them. I don't know how I would have reacted if the same had happened to me, but then I *had* been forced to take a part-time wage for a full-time job. Anyway, whatever I thought personally, it was my job to make this latest cost-cutting scheme happen. I couldn't think about the feelings of the people I was affecting.

It would have been nice to go home and sleep after doing a full day's work at night time, but I was much too paranoid about being absent from my office. Ever since my couple of days off for my 'family emergency,' Mike was already finding excuses to bypass me and go to Jason for management decisions on behalf of my team. If I didn't force myself back between them in the chain, I would be side-lined and effectively redundant.

That's why I was exhausted when Penelope asked to see me that afternoon. I counted up that I had actually been working for fifteen hours straight. My new found confidence seemed to have evaporated. I was annoyed to realise that once again I was petrified as I waited outside her office, convinced she was going to have a go at me for handling the night workers incorrectly somehow. Had I been too reasonable when giving them the bad news? Not "proactive" enough, whatever that means?

When she finally called me in, I had sweaty palms and the carpet in her office felt like some kind of gangplank over a shark-infested sea.

"Louisa, I'll come straight to the point," she said, ushering me into a chair with a languid flick of one wrist. "You would make an excellent HRBP."

I could hardly believe I'd heard right. A business partner? That would be a good promotion, higher profile with my hard work being more visible to the bigwigs, and making the next step up to Head of HR afterwards much more achievable. "Sorry?" I gulped.

"Oh yes, I have been aware of your potential for some time," Penelope breathed. Was that a flicker of a smile? Something in her face made me shiver. She held my gaze, and for the first time I noticed tiny flecks of yellow in those blue-green eyes.

Almost hypnotic.

"I'm sure the extra money would be useful?" she purred.

For a moment, I allowed myself to dream.

The job Sunna did seemed even harder than mine, and it was better paid. The Human Resources Business Partners were treated with a bit more respect than those of us that did the essential but less glamorous HR processing. It was a vague hope of mine to move into a vacant role alongside Sunna in a few years' time, maybe. I was too scared to think about any kind of future at GLC most of the time. Penelope kept us all feeling like progression was laughable, as we had to give all our time and energy just to wing it and stay in our current jobs.

I knew that one of the long-serving business partners, Frank, had recently retired and his post was still vacant. A promotion to his role for me would mean a minimum of an extra ten grand a year, overnight. I could help Manda with Joseph's treatment and still catch up with the money I had missed out on since going part-time. It would mean not having to worry financially. The prospect of that peace of mind was too good to turn down.

I pushed everything Sunna had warned me about out of my mind. The long hours, the guilt at being so cut-throat and destroying other people's dreams.

I wanted that money.

"So, are you advertising Frank's vacancy externally?" I asked. What I really wanted to know was, are you just going to give me the job or will I have to fight for it? Penelope had dished out promotions to favourites with no recruitment process before, though I had never been a favourite before so had had to work.

"Oh no, that post will be cut. Offered as a saving."

I was baffled. "Then, there aren't any vacancies at the moment?" The dream was slipping away. As I thought of Joseph's little face, I felt sick at the thought of the money I could have had to help him that seemed to be out of reach.

"There isn't a vacancy *yet*, Louisa," Penelope tutted, "but there *could* be. Dear Sunna shows no sign of recovery and has seemed rather unmotivated of late."

Sunna? "Is she still off sick?" I was panicking. I guessed she had allowed her hangover duvet days to continue regularly. Probably to make up for some of the extra hours she had been working, unpaid. "Penelope, I'm sure you don't need me to tell you we've got no right...not when a member of staff is off sick...we need to try to help her get better and come back..."

"She's not meeting her contractual obligations." Penny's tone was clipped and cold.

I wouldn't do it.

"She hasn't seemed happy in her work for some time." The menace in her tone belied the laughably caring sentiment of her words.

No.

She lowered her voice, forcing me into an intimacy with her and her lies, "I would like to give you this opportunity to shine." Penny gave me a strangely maternal look.

It was such twisted logic. She almost had me believing that this was a gift, rather than a perverse test of my loyalty. Would I sacrifice a really good friend, one of the few people who stood up for me at GLC, not to mention my own sense of ethics, to get ahead? Would I do whatever Penelope asked to keep my tenuous grip on a well-paid job?

I couldn't do it. I wouldn't do it.

"I'm afraid this conversation is making me a bit uncomfortable," I managed to mumble, flushing at being so assertive with Penelope of all people. "Perhaps I'd better get back to work now."

I had almost reached the door, when Penelope's voice, icy now, reached me like a slim blade between the shoulder blades.

"It's going to happen anyway, of course," she breathed.

I felt chilled to the core. I stopped and stared at her office door, one of her many CIPD awards framed on it.

Penelope's voice was rather hushed now, which had the effect of making it pierce more effectively into my horrified brain.

"It may be kinder for the news to come from…" she seemed amused or disgusted by the word, "a *friend*."

It was now clear how the land lay. If I didn't sack Sunna, Penelope would see to it that someone else did and would probably find an excuse to get rid of me, too. No pay raise for me, no extra money for Joseph.

And Sunna *had* said she was hating her job…

No. I wouldn't do it.

I fled to my desk. Ploughing through emails and rewriting my 'to do' list allowed me to slow my breathing and stop my hands from shaking.

Penelope didn't waste a second in punishing me for my insubordination. By the time I had been back at my desk for five minutes, I saw it. She had sent round one of her mass emails, copying in the Board and the Senior Management Team, giving the impression that my team's performance was down and I was the reason. As I read it, humiliation burned through me. I thought of all the people reading that email and felt so stupid and embarrassed. How dare she?

But I wouldn't betray my friend, no matter what Penelope did to me.

Chapter Twenty-Four

Thursday

Tossing and turning in my big empty bed, I was still awake at three in the morning. I hadn't slept at all for three nights and I was starting to feel desperate. Working through the night and doing a normal day of work on either side of it seemed to have thrown my sleeping pattern out altogether. I felt jet lagged. I felt so anxious, I couldn't get my brain to shut up and let me rest. I was going back over and over that awful conversation with Penelope asking me to stab Sunna in the back. I was worried about Sunna being destroyed by somebody else. I was petrified that Penny would now get *me* removed by another ambitious young thing.

My mind was racing with these conflicting demands that I just couldn't balance. I needed the money, I didn't want to behave in an unethical way, I wanted to do well, I felt I had no power and those who did were most definitely not on my side. And what about the plans for a restructure I had seen in Mike's inbox? When were we all going to have to compete for our jobs against outsiders? My thoughts went round and round.

I padded to the computer and logged on to the website of the counselling service I'd set up for GLC staff, looking for the phone number. I never thought I'd need it for myself.

I got through to a voicemail message. Someone would phone me back during office hours if I could give a brief description of the reason I wanted counselling. I didn't know how to explain this horrible feeling of dread, and a sense that I was wasting my life while systematically hurting those around me, so I hung up. I crawled into bed and then went in to work as soon as the merest grey light appeared on the horizon.

I stared at the pictures on my desk. I could see my face reflected, though I hardly recognised myself. Who had I become? I was constantly pre-occupied. I muttered to myself like a mad woman, hardly able to see the world around me. My experience of life felt shrunken down to a tiny narrow window onto the memory of the latest argument with Mike or point-scoring session courtesy of Penelope. I didn't sleep, though I over-ate.

I sat in my office and tackled a huge pile of work. No matter how ruthless I was about not taking on more than I could do in four days, there was always an overspill. My team couldn't get through the amount they needed to now their numbers had been so reduced. And there were always extra projects which Mike had been assigned by Penny which he had then delegated to me.

I knew I was getting run down and I never seemed to switch off. I had a weird out-of-body sensation all the time, and I knew I was getting worryingly slow at blitzing through the work. I was making silly mistakes and it would surely only be a matter of time before I slipped up badly.

By about nine, all my team had arrived and we were beavering away. I hadn't heard from Mike much for a few weeks and I was starting to get paranoid about it. Why wasn't he talking to me? What did he know that I didn't? Or my worst fear – was he discussing getting rid of me with Penny? The thought of losing my salary and not being able to help Joseph was unbearable. The shame of it, too, made me feel hot and sick. I was proud of being a professional. What else did I really have? My friends (not that I ever saw them) had husbands, children, homes they were making the way they wanted, but all I had was my career. Somehow in my head I had transplanted Penelope's horrible suggestion that I should take Sunna's job onto a different, shadowy plan in which I would be got rid of to make way for someone else. I trusted no one. The lack of sleep was making me less rational, I knew that, but I still wanted to know why the tense silence was surrounding me.

I logged into Mike's emails. Glancing down the subject lines, I noticed one from Rupert, titled "Project Louisa Can't." Seeing my name made my stomach drop horribly. A tiny voice in my jangled head told me that this was very bad news.

I opened the email. The body of the email from Rupert just read, "As discussed. Nice little earner." There was a document attached. I opened it, but it took its time to load.

Leigh banged gently on my glass office door. She signalled the question, "All right if I come in?" I nodded and she sat herself down, wearing a pretty maternity dress that flattered her rather heavy pear shape.

"Sorry, Louisa, I'm always in here moaning. It's just that I'm a bit worried about these extra duties Jason's been offered. He really appreciates the money but he's more stressed that he'll admit about not having enough experience. To be honest, he's panicking, but he'll never come to you and say anything; he doesn't want to let anyone down."

I looked at her blankly, "Sorry, Leigh, back up a minute. What extra duties are these?"

Now it was her turn to look baffled. "You know, the things Mike asked him to do. I assumed he'd let you know all about it?"

Mike. That idiot. I should have known. I won't be unprofessional, I thought, even though the seething feeling inside made me want to tell the world how pathetic Mike was. I hate making the team feel like there isn't a united front, though, giving the impression that management aren't talking to each other. "Maybe he's going to tell me today. I'll catch up with him about it. Then I'll meet Jason. Thanks for letting me know."

I gave her a smile and she looked relieved not to have caused trouble. "I mean, I'm ever so grateful he's being 'groomed' for promotion…" she continued.

I didn't hear any more of what she said. The document from Mike's emails had finally loaded. It was sixty-seven pages long and included lots of structure charts which had been clunky to load. I scanned it quickly.

It was a plan for my team and the rest of Shared Services. It showed costings of all our salaries, set against much cheaper equivalent salaries, with all the savings worked out. I scrolled down. That didn't make any sense? How could Rupert justify paying us all much less? A transfer of staff across different GLC sites was mentioned, and relocation costs... I scrolled back up to the introductory blurb. It couldn't be.

"Are you all right, Louisa?" Leigh broke in to my thoughts, "You look as if you've seen a ghost."

Falkirk was the new intended location for our services. This plan was about relocating Shared Services to Scotland. But transfer all of us up there? How could that be possible?

But I knew. Our contracts said we would work at any GLC site, and we had the tiny office not far from Glasgow – a historical throw-back we never thought about. With the law on their side, Rupert and Mike could force all of us to relocate, or else have put ourselves out of work, with no compensation whatsoever.

"So sorry, Leigh," I said weakly. "I'll have to catch up with you a bit later."

"Yes, of course," she was backing away, looking mortified to be dismissed by management.

I should have explained to her better. I should have summoned the energy to say, "Look, you haven't done anything wrong, I just want to give you my full attention, when I've dealt with this crisis," but I didn't. I let her go, my exhausted brain barely registering the hurt and confusion on her face.

I couldn't do this. I was too tired, too miserable. I had such reserves of good humour and nothing used to get me down, how had they managed this? I needed to be at home, with the curtains drawn. I couldn't speak to people, I couldn't meet their eyes. I stumbled through the banks of desks, not taking in the confused stares of my team, and forced myself to hold it together just enough to get myself home. Then I let myself cry.

Chapter Twenty-Five

Friday

I was so sick I couldn't stand. I was so sick I could barely see. But I had to get into work. No sick pay for the first eight days, how could I have been so stupid? Stupid for getting the policy through, stupid for letting myself get so tired and run-down, and stupid for still working for Penelope after vowing I'd get out so many times.

I tried to lift my head off the sofa. The phone was a short stagger away. But who could I call? I couldn't disturb Sunna again, and I felt uneasy about talking to her without fessing up about Penny's plans, which would be career suicide. I didn't want to worry my mum, who had been concerned about me working too hard ever since we spent a few days together. She didn't know that I hadn't taken a single day off since, not even weekends.

I had spoken to Mum earlier and it had taken all my strength to sound positive and normal. She's so different since Dad died. She's subtly more ready to agree, slightly less sure of herself. When I was growing up, I'd contradict her with some immature pronouncement, and she'd be this impenetrable wall of certainty. But these days, if I challenge her opinion on anything from the war on terror to feral children, she adopts a less confident manner, almost a "you're bound to be right" kind of frailty. It broke my heart, and there was no way I was going to burden her with my work-induced illness.

The person I wanted to talk to most was Liz. But where was she? Had she had to return home by now, or was she crashing at one of her waster friends' houses? We hadn't known each other when she had lived in South Africa so I had no phone number for her family there, and I knew that if she had gone back, she wouldn't have taken her English mobile with her. Email? Facebook? It felt so impersonal, and even if I did manage to get hold of her, she had every right to refuse to communicate with me. I was scared of her reaction.

But I wanted her there more than anyone. Even when I was looking at my most awful, she was the person I wanted to look after me. Wasn't that more important than my stupid career? Hadn't she told me as much?

Using every ounce of my strength, I lifted myself up onto my elbows and reached over as far as I could towards the house phone on its little table. My arms were shaking and juddering by the time I managed to grab it and cradle it in my arms. The receiver virtually slid out of my sweaty hands as I dialled Liz's mobile number, one I think I'll always know by heart.

Liz's phone rang seven times, then I heard her voice. A wave of nausea rushed through me as I heard her say the words, "Hi, this is Liz, I'm not around so please use the force or leave a message..."

I was so exhausted and disappointed, I virtually sobbed down the phone, "Liz, pick up, please, I feel like death, wherever you are please just get back to me, or come round, please – "

Then I hung up before I could further humiliate myself. Why should she answer? I was her ex, and possibly the only one of her exes who had got her sacked. I had no right to expect her to help me now.

My heart nearly stopped when the phone suddenly rang in my arms. I dropped the whole thing on the sofa like a bomb. "Gah." I grabbed the receiver and smacked it to my head which was already spinning.

"Liz? Thank God – "

"No, Louisa, it's Penelope," came the crisp voice at the other end. "How long will you be away on sickness absence?"

"My doctor thought a week at least," I groaned. "I'm really sorry."

"Just get yourself better, Louisa, and we'll have a catch-up when you are. I'll make use of occupational health to support you back to work."

PEOPLE PERSON

Oh, great. I knew all the tricks companies could legally use on a sick member of staff. "There's really no need –" But she had gone.

Chapter Twenty-Six

Monday

My doctor said I could go back for half time hours, which was now two days a week since I was already reduced from five days to four. The money would still not be enough to cover my rent and bills but it was more than the statutory sick pay which was all I had been receiving. The thought of going back to work was exhausting but I had to start somewhere. I was going to have to get back to work at some point.

I had tried to claim housing benefit but with Liz's name still on the tenancy agreement, the only way I could claim would be to prove she had gone by getting a letter from our landlady, and the benefit people could still make a surprise visit to count the toothbrushes in the bathroom. I just wasn't up to all that. It seemed easier to focus my slowly recovering energies on getting better.

Mike seemed reluctant to have me back when I phoned him to discuss the whole half-hours thing.

"My doctor doesn't have a problem with me coming in tomorrow. I'm feeling a bit better, and I don't want my work to slide any more than it already will have done."

"Don't rush back, Louise. Tomorrow's too soon."

That sounded odd. How would Mike know whether I was better or not? "I feel OK, Mike. The doctor's the expert, anyway."

"Sorry, Penelope wants you to see our Occ Health doctor and get the all clear from him first."

"That's mad. I don't mind seeing him, but in the meantime I need to get back to work. I've been signed back by my own GP so you're covered."

"Sorry. Nothing I can do, her mind is made up."

He was always using Penny as an excuse. How long was all this faffing going to take? When I'd used our Occ Health team in the past for sick employees, the appointments had had at least a two week waiting list. "Can I at least work from home until then? I really need the money."

"Well, I'll arrange for you to get paid for the two days a week until we've got the Occ Health report. Look out for their letter with an appointment." Then, click – he was gone.

The bastard had hung up on me. What the hell had gone on? Why had he been so reluctant to have me back in the building?

It was frustrating to be in this limbo, not allowed back to work, even though my GP had signed me back. It took ages to be seen by the cheap occupational health company GLC had cut corners by using. We used to have a doctor with an office on site, so you could see him when needed and be back at work the same day. But his post had been cut to make savings, and now we paid a private company to "health check" our staff – when they had time. Their other clients paid more; therefore we were always the lowest priority.

The appointment letter took a week to be sent through, and then the date of it wasn't for another two weeks after that. By the time they'd seen me and sent the report to Mike saying I was sort of better, the four weeks I was supposed to be working half time would be over. There was no way I could afford it to be extended – I needed to be getting full time money again as soon as possible or I would be screwed. I'd have to pretend I was back to full health and ready for four days a week, even though with no easing in period, the thought was a bit scary.

The morning I finally returned to work, I was so glad to see my team I didn't notice the changes right away.

Kimba had taken voluntary redundancy but she had popped in to visit Sian and Melanie as they raced around the reception area doing several jobs at once. They were polite to me, but an understandable change had happened to our relationship after everything the company had put them through.

Carly was sitting in my office. Trying to conceal my irritation, I breezed in.

"Hi, Carly."

She didn't budge from my seat. She even had my computer on, and was poring over a spreadsheet of some kind.

"...Are you waiting for me?" I asked, more impatient by the nanosecond. *Get out of my office.*

"...Hi, Louisa," she said distractedly, making it clear that she was too busy to talk to me. After another minute she said, "Penny just asked me to keep an eye on things while you were off...and get your team's performance stats together for her...."

I saw red then. "Jason is my deputy," I managed, in a low growl. "He 'keeps an eye on things' if I'm away. He's in charge."

Jason sloped up to the doorway, his face dark with annoyance. "That's what I said," he muttered to me, seemingly afraid that Carly might hear him.

"Just out of interest, Carly..." a nasty thought occurring to me. "How did you find time to hold the fort here, considering you're only in half the week? Has Hazel been looking after Penny while you were away?"

"Hazel's gone."

What? I knew Hazel needed her part-time job; there weren't any others to be had in Swinton. "What on earth made her go?" I had to ask, even though I knew the answer. The evil Carly had made her go, of course, egged on by Penelope.

"Oh, she'd been looking bored and miserable ever since she came back from mat leave," shrugged an unmoved Carly, hardly looking round. "I wanted to increase my hours to full time, and Penny could see I would give her better value."

There was no level the two of them wouldn't stoop to. Instead of feeling sorry for a new mum with post-natal depression, they had pushed her out of employment.

With a shake of the head to force myself to focus, I looked at the files Carly was calling up on my computer. Nosy little cow!

"And, anyway, I send our performance stats monthly to Mike, who shares them with Penelope at their meetings," I said loudly, trying to use body language to make her move without actually hurling her across the room. "So if Penny needs them again, get them from him."

"Apparently he hasn't been receiving the information from you."

Ooh that liar! Mike had said that I didn't give him the Board reports it took me days to put together each month? Presumably he hadn't understood them or had lost them or some incompetence, and had put the blame on me behind my back. "I've got all the monthly emails with dates showing when I sent them to him. And I've got all the 'read receipts,' too."

"Really?" She actually turned and faced me now. "Mike swore blind he hadn't been sent them. That's why I've had to start from scratch and put this spreadsheet together for the last year."

We looked at each other. As adversarial as our relationship was, for a moment we were united in horror. Mike had been caught telling a serious lie to Penny to cover up his own mistake. There was so much evidence this time; he was never going to get away with this one. It gave me quite an unpleasant shiver down the spine to think of the consequences. I was damned if I was going to take the blame for him when for once I actually had proof that he was lying to save his own skin.

Wrestling control of my computer from Carly, and charming her into standing aside even if I couldn't force her out of my office once and for all, I emailed Mike to gently ask him about what had gone wrong. He responded as he often did with a barrage of emails blaming everyone else, especially me.

Looking at Mike's string of angry emails, I realised he had never had a clue what was going on in the teams he was supposed to be managing. When something went wrong, he would distance himself from the relevant manager by sending them a critical email, copying in the Board and the Senior Management Team, saying how disgusted he was by what had been allowed to happen. He had got the idea from Penny – she always copied in all the bigwigs if she wanted to humiliate the recipient. But in Mike's case, he had no clue why it had happened, and therefore was powerless to prevent it from happening again. He managed in title only. It made me furious to think of his fat salary, posh company car, and cushy job. No one seemed to be checking up on him. No one seemed to question what he was doing all day. It made my blood boil.

"Look, Louisa," Carly was back to business now. "Penelope has got her talent management plan in place, it's all arranged. I learn your job so you can be promoted to Business Partner, help Sunna to improve and she may have a chance of applying for the Head of Shared Services vacancy."

I blinked. "What vacancy?"

"Well, Mike's job, of course. He's been a liability for years. You won't let him get away with all the things he's said about you over that time, will you?"

"But, what is Penny expecting me to…?"

"Well, obviously, Louisa," Carly was now taking no trouble to keep any respect in her voice. "As the Business Partner for his area, you would commence poor performance proceedings against him. He might improve…but if not, you would sack him. Leaves a space for Sunna, and for you, and for me. Everyone's happy."

So Penny had even kept her beloved henchwoman in the dark about Sunna. I guessed not a single one of us had the whole truth, in case of revolt. I was exhausted. I was sick. Maybe I had just got blasé about it all. I didn't even argue. I just told Carly, "OK, deal. But Jason needs a pay rise if he's not going to get my job after all. He's got a kid on the way. And Sunna will be fine; she is more than capable of moving up to the next level and she would do a much better job of running all the Shared Services than Mike would. She has been bored, that's all."

"And Mike himself?" Carly whispered with deadly precision.

"Leave him to me."

If anyone can, Louisa Cannes.

Chapter Twenty-Seven

I got Carly out of my office and closed the door to think.

I needed a chess board to work out all the politics at GLC at that moment.

So, where were we? It seemed that Mike had been trying to bad mouth me over the years I had worked for him to keep me in line and prevent me from progressing, but by some miracle, Penny had seen through this and wanted me to get rid of Mike. How did Jason fit into all of this? Why was it that he had been given these additional duties by Mike, and if Jason had been the one chosen to push me out, why was it that Penny had fielded Carly to replace me if necessary?

I was clearly missing a piece of the chess game. I picked up the phone to the Treasury Management team.

"Hello, can I speak to Rupert. Yes, it's urgent."

When he finally came on the line, I had to fight to keep my voice steady. That drawling, self-satisfied plummy accent.

"Louisa Can't?" he chuckled, clearly delighted with his childish nickname for me.

"You're a prick. Tell me, what's the situation with you and Jason? Why did you want to destroy him?"

"Don't get your knickers in a twist, little Louisa. I supposed that pussy has resigned, then?"

"Certainly not, Jason is back at work and doing very well. His injuries were awful but he is resilient and he has made a full recovery, physically at least."

Rupert seemed genuinely kind when he said, "Poor little Jason."

I was confused. Surely this wasn't remorse, at last, from a man who seemed only capable of harm and self-gratification?

"Well, yes," I said carefully. "He has been through a horrible experience, thanks to you, and nothing will make that OK, but perhaps if you did apologise to him, he would be able to get past it, eventually."

"Apologise?" The old Rupert was back, gleeful with derision. "I did the company a favour. He's a wuss, Louisa," now the compassionate tone was for me, and it made my blood boil. "I know in HR you like looking after wimps and losers, but in the real business world we need to know who is tough enough to survive. I tested the new boy, and showed everyone that he is a failure. Better we know that now, before he gets any more grooming for the top."

"Rupert, we need all kinds of people working here, not just posturing alpha males!" I was angry but also my stomach was crawling with insecurity. "And anyway, I wasn't particularly 'grooming Jason for the top,' as you put it, he was good at his job but he was still very young, not ready for more responsibility just yet."

"Oh dear, you are being cut out, aren't you," his voice was icy with triumph. "He was being groomed for *your* job, initially, silly Louisa. If he could demonstrate to Penny that he could manage without you, the plan was to scrap your post and then he would be proving himself for the next rung in the ladder in a couple of years. He was hungry, I'll give him that."

All my rage had dissipated, washed away by the chilly fear of losing my job.

So a fear I hadn't even thought realistic had been there all along, with no doubt the rest of the company aware and me being oblivious. I was too trusting, assuming that those around me would behave in a fair and decent way. But I had looked after my Jason, my loyal deputy, and all along he had been plotting with Mike to take my job?

I can't describe how fundamentally upsetting it was to me to feel my job was going to be taken off me before I was ready to go. It is a primal insecurity for me. My source of income, my status, my feeling needed. All gone because of some disloyalty and a half-baked plan to save a post on the structure chart?

PEOPLE PERSON

Focus, Louisa, I told myself. If you give in to this fear, then what? Are you going to run away and hide? Resign before they can sack you? My inner voice was saying: yes, flee. Leave behind all the stress and having to be tough. Go home and pull the covers over your head, where you are safe and life is easy.

But I didn't want to obey that voice. It was the voice of childishness, the voice of giving up. What are you made of, Louisa?

I slammed the phone down and mentally updated the pawns in Penny's chess game. She had given me a stark choice. Destroy Mike, control Jason, sack Sunna, and enter into an uneasy truce with the bitch Carly. Do these awful, unethical things, and maybe, just maybe, my job would be safe.

Sell my soul and gain the grudging respect of the woman who had us all on puppet strings.

But the photo of Joseph on my desk told me all I needed to know.

I had no choice.

Chapter Twenty-Eight

Tuesday

Mike looks hideous when he cries.

That fat smooth pink face blubbering, with the eyes cast down and the huge bulk of body slumped forward in his chair in defeat.

The poor performance documents had not taken long to pull together. I had so many examples of deadlines missed, responsibility shirked, and whole days wasted with sharing dodgy material and making inappropriate comments about colleagues to his stupid laddy mates via the company email. He had been too lazy or stupid to cover his tracks, and had made it easy to collect a damning dossier of evidence that he was just not up to the job.

I should have been feeling triumph, vindication, but all I felt was numbness. Even my own inner pep talk was not working. This man tried to get you sacked, Louisa! Fight back! Do the same to him! But I am not an unfair person. I do not like causing other people harm. Christ, how do I get off this path?

Penny sat alone, presiding over the meeting with an expression that suggested she could smell something slightly rancid. She had brought Carly along as a sort of poisonous little henchman, to take notes and generally put the boot in. I had been tasked with putting together the information that would deprive Mike of his income, his ability to get another job, and to ensure that his dignity would be in tatters before we had finished with him. My 'to do' list that week had read something like this: 1) sack Mike 2) stuff face with chocolate and ignore nausea.

I realised that Mike was pleading with me. I was horrified and a little ashamed of the power I wielded. But I couldn't stop. Wasn't I getting paid a fortune to do shitty things like this? Wasn't I being an HR bitch: impressive, don't-mess-with-me, powerful?

With most people, you had to use a bit of psychology to work out their weaknesses, but in Mike's case, they were glaring. Dennis was his rep, and he did his best for Mike, but there was no defence they could come up with. His behaviour had been inexcusable. Instead Dennis focused on reminders about the impact Mike losing his job would have on his wife, children, and mortgage, while pointing out how difficult it would prove for Mike to find another job at his age. Penelope reminded me when we were alone in adjournments that these points about the human cost of his sacking, "had absolutely *no bearing* whatsoever on the case."

I was inclined to agree with her, in principle, but some sort of human compassion kicks in when you are confronted with a person in need. I supposed I had to admire Penny's entirely cold and logical approach to justice.

She didn't attend for the outcome, saying it was appropriate for me to act for the organisation while sacking Mike. While I found the crying uncomfortable and I felt quite guilty when Mike's wife came to collect him, looking so middle-aged and defeated in her anorak and sensible shoes, I still told myself that I had done the right thing. The organisation was flabby, Mike was a chancer, and he had never worked hard enough or been talented enough to deserve that job. I would do it better, and I did.

So, Mike left and I became the new Mike. Sunna was quietly exited from GLC, not even a farewell party, just a note on the Marketing team newsletter under the heading, "Colleagues who leave the company this month." I didn't even pick up the phone to her, as my newly increased pay and responsibilities depended not just on her business partner role being scrapped, but also on my public loyalty to Penny.

What a bizarre turn of events. My life seemed to be a particularly cruel and twisted joke these days. I had to laugh at the things I found myself doing and the person I had become.

PEOPLE PERSON

At first I just took on most of the extra duties and returned to working full time for no extra money, but after a few days word came from Penelope, via Carly, that I was to change my job title to "Head of Shared Services" and would receive a small pay raise (nothing compared with what Mike had been on, but still.) It was a saving overall to the organisation; particularly as I took the trouble to find out what people actually wanted and ended up working much longer hours than Mike ever had. People started to come and say to me that they had never really understood what Mike did or even asked me whether this was a new post, confirming my suspicions that Mike had been deliberately hiding in his office to avoid work from coming his way. All around, I was telling myself to feel pretty victorious and good about myself in a grown-up, professional way. I had taken a tough decision, it had been the right thing to do, and I felt I deserved the promotion and pay raise I'd got out of it.

It was just that I had the nagging feeling that this was someone else's life, and my own was passing me by.

Chapter Twenty-Nine

Wednesday

My first priority after taking over Mike's job was to rebuild my shattered team. We had been turned against one another, and I could either let that carry on until the environment became toxic, or I could be the bigger person and start the bridge-building. I took Jason out for lunch in the pub we always go to. I knew him well enough to be direct.

"How long have you been gunning for my job?" I asked him.

He choked slightly on the piece of bread he was chomping while he waited for his steak and chips.

"Boss?" he stuttered, visibly pale.

"Look Jase, I know Mike was stirring and trying to get you to compete with me. He probably made you feel like it was the best way to get some extra money for the baby, am I right?"

Jason looked incredibly uncomfortable. "Yep," he managed.

"But listen, you and I have always been on the same team, and I can get you a raise now. I need you to step up and take over the role I used to do, or most of it, because I can't do all the running of our staff and also the stuff Mike was supposed to do."

I waited while he recovered, giving him time to think through his options. I needed to know whether he was loyal to me or not. There were a number of secrets I needed to share with him, but only once I knew for sure whether he was in or out.

"Louisa, I am so sorry," he stumbled. "I felt really bad about it at the time, it was just that Mike was so convincing about how you were struggling and you would probably just resign at some point anyway...."

I had to put a finger over my mouth to stop myself from ranting about that Mike, the worst boss in the world, how *dare* he....

"So I just did my best to do all the extra work he was asking for, but I guess that is pretty much what I'll need to do for you now?"

I breathed out. "You're right, that is what I'll need you to do for me, eventually. But first, we will have to do a little firefighting."

I glanced around at the quiet pub. I couldn't see anyone from work.

I leaned in and lowered my voice, "I'm going to show you some emails now that I'm not supposed to have. Read them and then I'm going to shred them. Don't react."

He looked nervous about my cloak and dagger approach, but he kept calm while I slid the small sheaf of papers out of my bag.

I continued to scan the pub while he read through my dossier. The emails between Mike and Rupert about the savings they could achieve by replacing most of my staff with a call centre in Falkirk, paying the staff there a pittance even by local standards, using the most cynical of contracts with no security or dignity. In addition to this was the Board paper where Penny had detailed her plan to make this work, including the loop hole in all our contracts that meant we would be expected to relocate to Scotland to carry out these worse-paid jobs or else voluntarily resign and walk away from the security of jobs with many years of loyal service, yet not be entitled to a penny in redundancy compensation. Penny had explained in her plans that we would have to compete for our jobs against applicants from the local area of Falkirk, and there would be a small handful of roles still needed at our current site in Swinton, so that for those who wished to remain, again there would be a straight fight between us, up against any new applicants who chose to apply for our jobs. Oh, and to top it all off, the very few of us who managed to be successful would not remain on our current salaries but would have to accept new terms that were considerably worse, including a change to one year fixed term contracts with no guarantee of a job after that.

PEOPLE PERSON

Jason was looking very pale, even for him, *"No..."* Both he and Leigh would be affected, along with all their friends and confidantes. Our team were like a family. All the local kids came to work in our teams. This felt like such an attack on our little community.

"So what do we do about this?" Jason asked, shoving the last of the documents aside. He was looking less afraid now and more pissed off.

Good. Anger was good. We were going to need that.

"We can't take on the Board, neither of us would be listened to at that level," I began. "And we can't hobble Penny; she stands to gain too much from this. With Mike out of the picture, the only weak link I can think of is Rupert. He's lazy, so he's less likely to have done his homework properly. If we can find a flaw in these proposals which seem to have been his idea, we might be able to fight back and embarrass him enough to get him to back-track on these plans."

"We could get the local press involved," said Jason, grimly. "This isn't going to look good, a large company taking away local jobs."

"Yes, I suspect Penny is very keen to keep this story away from the press until it's too late," I whispered. I could feel a fire growing in the pit of my stomach. "What a brilliant feeling it will be to leak this at just the worst possible moment for her."

I was terrified, but this felt like the greatest reason to be working. A purpose, a cause, making the paper pushing I had been doing before seem like such a waste of my life. This time I would be working tirelessly to achieve something real, to stand up for people I cared about.

I didn't know whether we had what it took to win through, but I was going to give it everything I had.

Chapter Thirty

Thursday

Even though technically I was still easing back into work gradually after being ill, I was working even more hours than before doing Mike's old job and organising our fight back against the relocation. There had been no announcement yet but I wanted us to be ready, and I had to get enough people on our side for our voices to be heard.

I went into HR in the first place to make a difference. I couldn't get motivated by just making a profit for some businessman at the top of the pyramid. I wanted to contribute to the community I'd grown up in. But with the reputation my profession had now, sometimes I wish I hadn't bothered. The press love to give the impression that there are weird laws that mean businesses have to pay out too much money and can't get the changes done that they need to. Somehow the reputation of the personnel team in most companies are of a group of female staff who obstruct management decisions, blocking you from dealing with people in cushy jobs who are inefficient but can never be got rid of until they retire.

The truth is that if you get the right advice and aren't scared to get started, the law does allow a busy manager to take action and make sure staff improve or leave. What you actually do get is a steady stream of "new broom" managers coming in, all keen to get more done and change everything, and they'd bully the long-serving staff who were actually doing reliable work at a reasonable rate and had stuck around long enough not to make rookie errors. The manager would be trying to make their mark, and get promoted within one or two years, so actually it was the long-serving staff who provided the consistency to the customers.

And Personnel used to intervene, stick up for them and get the manager to be fair and humane, see the good that their staff were doing rather than focusing on getting them to do even more. These days though, it's HR that does the bullying. HR can be so hard-hearted, the manager might even be quite shocked by their methods and not ask for their advice with a plodding member of staff. They feel protective of what might happen to them if HR were to get involved.

Rupert, as one of these "new broom" managers, had hatched a plan to make savings by outsourcing most of Shared Services to a call centre in Falkirk, and Penelope had clearly loved the idea and was moving it through by stealth. And I did something I hadn't known I could. I organised a protest about it. We went door to door round the local estates, with posters to go in windows, and a petition. Leigh and Jason came with me. "Keep GLC services local – 'No' to foreign call centres." It wasn't xenophobia or even simple self-interest at the fact we would all lose our jobs if we refused to relocate to Scotland. It was about the loss of the quality of service you got here. It was something I really believed in, having trained and managed our staff. The offshore call centre would be staffed by people who had not grown up with GLC services and who would be reading scripts rather than getting all the training our guys did.

For the first time in a very long time, I felt my dad would have been proud of me.

Penelope demanded to see me in a private meeting. I was pretty sure that any meeting with her at this point would consist of a session of her badgering me to stop spreading rumours about her getting rid of local staff and moving the work we did to some far-away call centre. I told her I could only attend if I brought someone with me, preferably Dennis, our union rep. She backed down and cancelled the meeting. I knew it would only be a matter of time before she would find some other way to crush me, but in the short term it was round one to me and

PEOPLE PERSON

I needed to keep on fighting as quickly as I could before I could be silenced.

After work, I organised Leigh, Jason and a couple of the others from the team to drum up support for our campaign around the local streets, the church, and our local pub. I had explained to them the weakness in the plan which was to do with the long-serving staff who were on an old version of the contracts of employment, without the all-important clause that forced them to work at any site. Rupert didn't know this. He hadn't bothered to talk to any GLC employees he considered "old school", but I had, and I made sure the message was out there that the forced move would be against the law for some. We finished up there most nights, exhausted and discouraged from the apathy we often came up against. For every one person prepared to sign our petition and put one of our stickers in their window, there seemed to be another ten who couldn't be bothered to help as they weren't directly affected.

We were just having a few cold beers at the end of one such night of door-knocking when Leigh dug me in the ribs, "Isn't that Mike over there?"

"No, can't be," I stuttered, whirling round.

But it was.

Mike was horribly, horribly drunk.

He had the dazed, angry look of someone who had beaten out their brain with vodka and was looking for someone to blame it on.

"My wife thinks I'm at work," he snarled. "I couldn't bear her face every day, so I pretended I'd got one of the jobs I keep applying for. No one wants me though. Thank God I've never let her look at the finances or she'd see we're really eating into our savings."

"You'll find something, Mike," I tried to reassure him.

"Oh, little Louise." He leaned close and I drew back in my chair without meaning to. His breath was rank and boozy, "Pray you'll always be the latest thing. The young, lean, hungry generation." He started to almost chant at me, in a weird, sing-song voice. "Always in demand, always welcomed and given money. I used to be *just like you*," he chanted the last three words, poking his finger uncomfortably close to my face on each syllable. "Well, my luck's run out, hasn't it? Just pray the same thing doesn't happen to you, Tiger." His old pet name for me came out like a curse. He made an unlikely gypsy, but I felt something like a cold shudder despite myself.

The dank little old-man's pub had a wet-carpet smell and a look of desperation. It seemed to come from the patrons. Several men of Mike's age sat individually, drowning their sorrows. For a fleeting moment I wondered why they didn't all get together at one table and at least talk about the torment they were going through. Besides the men, there was one young girl with a pushchair, solemnly feeding her baby chips. The bar-staff looked as if they were attending a funeral.

"Mike, listen to me. You'll find something else, you'll get through this...."

"Hah."

"Have you tried retail? A store manager job, or heck, even a salesman position, just till you get back on your feet. Surely Penelope will give you a good reference...?" I knew the answer to that one in the downward tilt of his head. He was washed-up, finished. And it was all my fault. I remembered Sam, whose job I had been so cavalier with such a long time ago. I had hardly let myself think about the impact it would have on her. I wondered whether she had found work yet.

Mike staggered off to get home to his wife and I returned to my little band of followers.

"How is he?" Jason asked, nervously.

"Oh, fine," I lied. "Just popped in for a swift half, off home now." My guilt at destroying the careers of three people was weighing heavy on my heart. As I looked at the trusting little faces of my staff, I realised that I owed it to them to give up this fight. Penelope would win as she always did, and then she would make us all pay.

Chapter Thirty-One

Friday

I marched in to Penny's office without an appointment. This was one of the few advantages of Carly hanging out in my office all the time now, trying to get my staff on side. There was no poisonous henchman to keep the rebels like me away from the ice queen in her corporate castle.

Penelope Ross barely raised an eyebrow when she saw me stroll in without the fear I always used to show. On the contrary, she seemed to have anticipated this showdown.

I reflected on my purpose that day as I looked into those cold eyes. For some senior managers, you can tell that they are a figurehead and the real power lies behind the throne in the form of a deputy or a team of hard-working specialists. But in the case of Penny, all the power was on the throne, in every cell of her body. If you looked behind the throne, all you would find would be more power, and it would all be hers.

If I didn't get on with it quickly I would lose my nerve, "I'm no doubt causing an embarrassment to GLC, protesting about the Falkirk relocation, as one of your senior HR team?"

Penny gave a little snigger that sounded like the hiss of a serpent, "You are embarrassing yourself, Louisa, and your behaviour only reflects on yourself as a professional."

"Supposing I stopped?" I asked her. "Made all the protesting and petitions go away? As a trade, would you save the jobs of a handful of my staff, chosen by me? Jason, Leigh?"

"I really couldn't care less, either way," she spat.

"So you give your permission for me to continue? Escalate the action, get the press involved?"

"Is that supposed to be some sort of threat?" her voice was dangerously soft.

"I just thought that there were some stories that you would rather not hit the local headlines. Such silliness, really, but these rags do like a bit of gossip, particularly at the expense of bosses who are making ordinary workers suffer."

"Such as?" Penny looked supremely bored. She really hadn't thought of my trump card, at all.

"Your boyfriend beat up a member of staff. Your violent boyfriend, who still has a live police caution for sexually assaulting you, Penny."

She gave a blink.

I couldn't believe that I had been so nasty and neither could she. I had chosen to go there. At last, she had succeeded into turning me into her handmaiden of evil. Mini-me evil. Evil Junior, being groomed for the top. I had finally let her ruthless, sadistic methods change me, but I was using them on her. I had turned against my leader and was threatening to destroy her with her own weapons.

"Make sure this list of staff have jobs here." I let the piece of paper I had been holding flutter onto her desk. "For as long as they work at GLC, I will keep your secret safe."

She was looking at the list, gripping her hands together until her knuckles were white.

"I don't care what you do to me, but I will refer to my copy of this list. Daily. For the rest of my life, or yours, whichever is shorter. As soon as I hear that any one of my friends has been made redundant, I will give the local press a copy of the charge sheet, giving all the details of how Rupert assaulted you, and for how long, and with what. And I will ensure that the papers publish every humiliating detail, about how he took advantage of your adorable vulnerability while injured." I forced myself to look in her eyes, "I will do it, Penny. Do not have any doubt."

Then I left her office, doing my best to pretend I couldn't see her tears.

Chapter Thirty-Two

Monday

A letter was lying on my desk when I arrived at work after the weekend. On the front was written: "Louisa Cannes, Private and Confidential" in Rupert's backward sloping hand. I tore it open and sat down to read it. The letter started to shake in my hand. I was so *angry*.

"Dear Louisa," it read. "It has come to my attention that you have made the following errors recently in your work." Listed were some trivial mix-ups, most of which had not been my fault. The final paragraph read, "I would like to discuss these at a meeting tomorrow morning at 10am. To help you to prepare for this meeting, I have to inform you that I am minded to discuss how to end your employment at GLC. Yours sincerely, Rupert Carter-Hayes."

I shouldn't have been surprised, but I was. I was gobsmacked. They were pushing me out with no process, no fair hearing, just some manufactured 'performance issues' and a cosy meeting with Rupert. He was clearly acting under Penny's instructions: that last sentence couldn't have sounded more like her style. But Rupert didn't seem to have had the sense to get her to check the letter, or to take any HR or employment law advice. You can't just suddenly cook up a meeting and sack someone for some minor mistakes. GLC had a policy for performance management; I should know, I had to update it as one of my first tasks in my new role. The manager should bring the concerns to my attention and set a period of several months to allow me to improve. It wasn't as if any of these so-called mistakes were bad enough for me to get sacked on the spot. There was no evidence of any training they had given me, and if I had been advising from an HR point of view, I would have wanted to be sure that the line manager had given clear instructions what exactly he had wanted his staff member to do. The thought they could find even a Post-It note of clear instruction from Mike was laughable. Also, for a meeting where I could lose my job, Rupert had forgotten to tell me I could bring a representative.

All of this was good ammo but it didn't change the fact that it looked like I was unwanted at GLC. If they wanted to get me out, they would. There were huge disadvantages for the employee in this situation. Performance being assessed is one of the most subjective things unless your job involves something that can be compared with a model, like say assembly in a factory. How do you check how well an HR Manager is performing? Working with people is an evolving, mysterious thing. You could attribute staff complaints to the person making tough choices or to them being insensitive. A decent line manager would have looked at whether overall I was achieving what the company needed. There would have been correction along the way if I had been messing up. I couldn't think of a single useful bit of management advice from Mike. He had never once said that I should have done something differently, except for when Penny had been in his office raising hell.

But what could I really gain by telling them all this? They might have delayed the inevitable sacking. They might have set a review period and I would have had to toe the line. I knew I would be set up to fail. Penny would ensure she set such impossible standards that I would, on paper, have demonstrated my own "incompetence." Just like Sam and all the others.

Anyone being scrutinised under a performance management process was liable to go to pieces and start making mistakes they wouldn't normally. And did I really want to go through all that horrible time of being made to feel rubbish at my job? Besides, I needed to find another job, and the last thing I wanted was a bad reference. At least at this stage, my record had been unblemished until these recent so-called "errors," which I could show were not my fault.

PEOPLE PERSON

It was best for me if I quickly left now, before Penny and Rupert had a chance to blacken my name.

It was a trap I had spent the last year creating for myself. Shit. I kicked the base of my desk and yelped with pain. I hobbled around my office for a few minutes with my foot in my hands.

Chapter Thirty-Three

Tuesday

So I did leave, as they knew I would. I had been used to do Penny's dirty work and had been disposed of in less than a year.

Carly was the lucky upstart who got to process me, and hold my "off the record" conversation. You know, the one that starts with her doing a little frown of mock concern, and saying, "I know you haven't been *happy* here for some time…" Brilliant for her CV. I looked at her with new eyes. She seemed almost drunk with happiness at being singled out for the honour of getting rid of me. She even had the cheek to produce some "internal customer feedback" from the Finance department, no doubt coached by their aggressive boss, Rupert. I produced the emails he had sent Mike, with the pathetic subject line describing me as "Louisa Can't", and she had to grudgingly back down. That kind of email from a senior manager was alone grounds for a constructive dismissal claim and they knew it. I was holding out for a settlement.

I couldn't even feel angry with the little bitch, because there was no getting away from the fact that she was me, a year ago. I gazed at her prettily made-up face, all five foot nothing of her giving me earnest smiles across the desk in the interview room. I wondered whether she would be in exactly the same position as me in another year's time, being sacked by some brand new hopeful, breathlessly managing Carly's downfall.

I threw everything I could think of at them. I knew I had to leave but I didn't see why I should make life easy for them by slinking away without a fight. I reminded her that I was working part-time and there is legislation to stop them from disadvantaging me. I provided the numerous documents I had to prove that Mike's leadership had been confusing or non-existent. I got my doctor to write in with the effect the stress and long-hours had had on my health, something that had never happened in any of my previous jobs. Penny had come up with half-truths and out of context "examples" of my lack of brilliance, and made a fair stab at discrediting me through Carly as her evil little minion, but I knew I had a strong case and they were nervous. I was holding out for a payment. I wanted six months' salary if I was going to give up my well-paid job simply because I wouldn't play ball with a dishonest and nasty regime. In the end I got eight months' worth, if I would sign to say I wouldn't sue and would never breathe a word of what had gone on. It was more money than I'd ever seen before, and it gave me a few months' breathing space. Knowing the rent was paid for a while and I could afford to spend some time at home thinking my own thoughts and choosing how I directed my energy was like nothing I'd experienced since childhood.

Chapter Thirty-Four

Wednesday

So here I am. On my sofa in my pyjamas, being myself. I was lucky enough to reconnect with the person I am when left to my own devices.

The quality of my thoughts improved. I don't know how else to describe it. I returned to the positive, creative person I'd always been. The unpleasantness of GLC washed away and I was able to see it as a time where I'd learnt a heck of a lot about myself. There is something about extreme pressure which brings out the worst in a person, I think. Stress sharpens your weaknesses, forces you to behave in ways that would appal you in times of plenty. The mask of civilisation is a thin one at best, and I had faced myself when the mask had not only slipped but fallen to the floor and smashed, never to be re-affixed.

I realised that I had been defining myself in terms of my career, specifically my job title and my salary. I had loved to introduce myself and say what I did. Now I was unemployed, who was I exactly? Louisa. Louisa Cannes. Sitting in my lounge in my bathrobe watching daytime TV, I wasn't a success, I wasn't anybody special. I was just a slob, relaxing and being a human being. Being myself. At first it freaked me out, but as the days went by and I relaxed into it, I started to get a sneaking suspicion that it might actually be good for me. And get this – I started to lose weight. It was falling off me. Instead of stuffing my face to lift my spirits, I ate when I was hungry, and I had physical energy for the first time in years. I woke up feeling happy, and I was back in my old jeans. My stomach was flat and my hips were shrinking.

Now I had had my flashy job title taken away, what did I really want to do with my life? How did I want to spend each day?

Amanda's brush with ill-health had given me a real wake-up call, too. Anyone could become really sick, out of the blue, and then your own mortality makes you reassess your priorities. If I found out I only had six months to live, what would I want to get done?

I cooked, I cleaned, I made a list of friends I had been neglecting, and visited each one in turn. And…I phoned Liz.

On a hunch, I had spoken to David at work who had been speaking to Liz on Call of Duty. The ridiculous headset and the multi-player option against young lads without girlfriends had actually been my way of tracking her down. It turned out she had been staying at the South African pub in Aylham and was working there. I hadn't even thought of looking for her in this country. I suppose I couldn't imagine people thinking of *me* as decent and nice enough to put me up rent-free, even temporarily, and I had been judging her by my standards. But my lovely Liz had never harmed anyone else, never compromised her integrity, and when she needed help, people who knew her wanted to repay her kindness.

I asked her if she'd be prepared to come to the flat just to talk. She agreed and turned up forty minutes later. She looked as if she had run all the way. I had planned to give her breathing room, just maturely let her know I wanted to give things another try and see how she reacted. As soon as she walked in the door, she put her arms around me and scooped me up, and I burst into tears. So much for the mature, rational discussion.

"God, I've missed you so much," I sobbed into her hair.

"Shh-hh" she soothed.

"And I've lost my job!" I squeaked. "I've got nothing to offer you – I can't even pay the rent."

"No more GLC?" Liz looked at me. Her eyes were shining.

"They were awful, they didn't want me anymore. I had to leave."

"That's the best news I've had in a long time," she carried on, picking me up and swinging me round.

"Liz!"

"I'm serious! That place was no good for you, my love. You'll get a much better job, somewhere where you're appreciated. You won't be the stress monster anymore."

"I was never a monster!"

She didn't even have to respond to that one. We both knew it was true. I had been such a cow to her.

"Anyway, you always wanted your own business," she reminded me. "Now's as good a time as any to give it a go, right?"

I had forgotten it had always been my dream to do things my own way.

Liz got some dinner on while I sat at the rickety desk I'd put in the corner of the bedroom once when I had decided I wanted to work from home more often. Penelope had put a stop to that dream, too.

Blinking back tears, I started to fill in the business plan template I had kept in a box of old work stuff for years. I had forgotten it was there. An HR consultant had told me years ago that she had used it to help her set up her own business. It was a series of questions you answered to give you a set of values you wanted to work to.

I read the first one. What makes your business different?

I thought about the humiliating mass emails Penelope sent out. I thought about how staff had been casually got rid of, like cannon fodder in a pointless war. And I thought of Mike, drunk and defeated. He had been a breadwinner like me, cast on the scrapheap while his family panicked – Sam, ditto. Had I really done that to her? How could I ever forgive myself for behaving in such an unethical way?

And then it came pouring out of me.

I wrote, "Our ethical HR consultancy is different because we believe that human beings at work deserve to be cherished and treated with respect. We believe that it is their skills and opinions that make a business great. Where staff are treated well, like adults who are valuable to the company, the organisation benefits, because those staff members give their additional effort and go the extra mile."

This was easier than I had thought. I had a clear idea of my business already. A little flutter of excitement told me I could dare to believe this was possible.

I read the next question. What do you offer?

I considered this. Recently I had been thinking about the things I was good at, rather than the things I made myself do to fit in and earn money. So I started there. I wrote: "The things I'm good at, which are mediation, team building…" Suddenly an image of an advertising flyer flashed into my head, so I quickly sketched it out. I wrote a title, "Troubled Waters? We can help…" and at the bottom I wrote, "10% of profits goes straight to Joseph's Foundation, for children born with congenital heart defects." I was more excited about this project than I had been about work for ages, years maybe. I had gone into HR in the first place because it seemed like a way of looking after people who were working hard. And although the thought of not having a manager and making all my own decisions was a scary one, it was also exhilarating. I was going to work for myself. No one could make me do another unethical thing. No one could get rid of me just because I stood up to them or my face didn't fit.

Liz came in and was beaming at my enthusiasm. "Aren't you adorable when you're happy," she smiled, ruffling my hair. "What do you want for dinner – something healthy or something naughty?"

"Healthy, please. Vegetable soup maybe, or a chicken and salad sandwich? I could stand to lose a few pounds, and with all the new business that will be coming my way, I'm going to need maximum energy levels." Nothing like thinking positive.

If anyone can, Louisa Cannes.

~ THE END ~

About Alex Spear

Alex Spear loves traveling the world listening for stories. Born in London, she now lives with her wife by the sea. Many, many decades have passed since Alex was at school but she still gets told off for being easily distracted. She will typically be writing two novels, a blog and a TV script all at once while reading half a dozen novels (none from beginning to end) while talking to good friends online, on the phone, and to her cat. Alex says, "I am passionate about women and my mission is to tell our stories. The power of female relationships, from friendships to love affairs and everything in between, is the true history of the world. I want women to enjoy themselves more, and to look after themselves at least as well as they do everyone else."

If you have enjoyed **PEOPLE PERSON**
please look for ALEX SPEAR's novel **OUT** from
Shadoe Publishing:
We have a chapter here for your enjoyment.

PART ONE

I had entirely forgotten how to dance, but I only had to follow her.
She could dance for both of us.

Simoine de Beauvouir
The Blood of Others

Standing outside the clinic, making sure I couldn't be seen, I turned
my phone back on, and frowned. Missed call? I checked the number:
House Phone. Before I could even return the call, my phone buzzed
and flashed into life again, and it was Colin. My stomach dropped
when I heard his voice. Colin, the control freak, always in charge,
sounded like he was out of his mind with terror.

"Colin? What's the – "

"Lydia? Half the house has just – oh, God, it's so awful – "

"What? What's happened?" With a furtive look round, I ran to get
away from the ambulance sirens.

Colin's voice was stretched with panic. "Where are you, Lydia? I
didn't know where anyone was, I didn't know what to do..."

I hesitated, not wanting to lie. "Tell you later. What is it, though?"

"The crazy room – Sarah's room – it's fallen down. It's just
collapsed."

Chapter One

She looked terrified. I have that effect.

Lydia was flushed with embarrassment, right down over the neck and possibly as far as her tiny breasts. She had the kind of bone-white skin that often flares with eczema or mottles with freckles, but she had neither.

She must have grabbed the towel when I had knocked on her door. Her white, English body was wrapped in holiday colours: flamingo pink, banana palm green, tequila sunset orange.

"Have you looked at many others?" she was asking.

"None so cheap." Only the slightest creping below the collar bone to show she was no longer in her teens. Proper woman's stomach, not too flat. "Can I see it?"

"Oh, yes, of course!" She made for the stairs.

I dropped my sports bag in the hallway, which was actually one side of the very small lounge, in the very small house. I pushed my bag gently against the flaking radiator. The bag contained my life, or what was left of it.

She was half-way up the narrow staircase. Her bottom was obligingly outlined by the clinging velour. "Or did you want a cup of tea first, Sarah?" She paused and looked over her shoulder; a slender, porcelain doll wearing an ice-lolly wrapper.

Tea?

The banisters gave a chipboard wobble and she pulled her hand away as if from a stove.

Why was she stalling?

Of course. Suddenly, I understood her nerves, her rush to the door to let me in. The room was cheap, and she was desperate. It was going to be another dump. The three I'd seen that morning had been all but uninhabitable, and I'd been working down in price. This was the only one I could really afford. Dear God. How did I let things get so tragic?

"Nah. Let's see it."

We climbed to the phone box-sized landing together and she opened one of the four doors, singing out far too loudly, "there you go! Have a good look round! What do you think!" She stood aside to let me go in.

I could see why. This room ain't big enough for the both of us, sweet Lydia. It was really no bigger than the mean bed and MDF wardrobe pressed against the foot. (Do those doors even open?)

The room wasn't just far too small for sensible human occupation, it was also insane. By some deranged lack of planning or complete incompetence in the building, the walls were all at completely different gradients, not one of them perpendicular with the ceiling. You could have placed a marble in the doorway and it would have rolled miserably under the bed to the wall. Also, the reek of damp was as sharp as horse urine.

But.

The light.

Oh, the light.

The far wall was mostly window, apart from the mouldy lower third. There was another window in the right hand wall, which I calculated must be the end-of-terrace outside wall. Ancient crickle windows with rusted frames, bubbled with years of repainting. The room seemed to be more window than wall. It was a glasshouse, an observatory. To be in that room was to be bathed in the real light shining on this cruel planet. It was church when Jesus shows up.

I knelt on the bed and worshipped that view.

The view was postage-stamp gardens, plastic slides and black sacks. It was concrete roofs, it was estate walkways and the canal towpath furnished with street drinkers. It was a gang of kids on bikes, shouting and wheeling. It contained not a single tree. It was people. Life, community, other people, other people…I was exhausted by the sight of it already, yet desperate to watch it and watch it.

I've been alone for so long.

OK, easy there, Sarah. I wiped my eyes, quickly, knuckles dragged across before she could see.

"I'll take it," I growled, as she danced and shrieked in the background.

* * * * *

We had a real problem renting out the fourth room. It was built at crazy angles, and the same could be said of the last three tenants. Skanky Oliver rented the room a year, during which time, small explosions and smoke would emanate, until the summer day he disappeared. We broke the door down in the end, to find nothing but two empty suitcases, the bed up against the wall and on the stained carpet, the remnants of a modest but workable speed factory.

The second tenant we got in was a timid, intensely boring vegan girl. She filled our fridge with soya milk and sprouting mung beans, and woke us all up with her mad phone calls in the middle of the night. Christ knows who she rang. She spent hours at a time crying and going on and on about her guilt complex, her delicate and terribly complicated psyche. In the end, Pip had to ask her to go. Me and Colin kept out of it; we stayed in the kitchen while Pip sat her down in the lounge and gently explained that it wasn't working out. Pip's good at things like that. Besides, I had complicated matters by sleeping with the vegan a couple of times. I forget her name.

She had convictions, that was my downfall. What is it about a person so sure of their beliefs, that transforms them into the sexiest thing on earth? If I'm honest, it's butch women I really fancy, but it's pretty embarrassing admitting that these days. These days, even clinging resolutely to the old dyke uniform is kind of a fringe belief system, and it does things to me.

But a proper butch dyke is so hard to find, especially among girls of my age. It's like, you can be a lesbian, if you must, but you have to be feminine. At the very least you have to 'make the most of yourself.' Be honest, when is the last time you saw a butch lesbian on TV? They should be on the endangered species list. It won't be long before the last few get Gok Wang'ed or whatever, and I'll have no-one left to fall in love with.

The most recent tenant was a big biker guy, all leathers and body hair. He stayed a week, then got back together with his boyfriend, and left.

The crazy room stood empty, filled with light from the excessive windows, daring us to fill it again. We were really behind with the rent by now.

One night we were all in the lounge drinking, the way we do, when she rang. I grabbed the phone. Her voice was classic dyke: authoritative, cocky, with masculine inflection. Very crisp 'Ss. That kind of voice makes me go weak. I collapsed back into the chair with the phone cradled tenderly to my ear.

She said her name was Sarah. "I need a place to stay, very cheap."

"Where were you before, Sarah?" I did my best husky voice.

Our two kittens were fighting under the table. Jasper and Conran. I didn't name them, by the way.

For a second I thought she'd hung up. Then she did a bitter little laugh. "I...I lived with my partner, in her house, I mean. She died last year. Her parents took back the house and threw me out."

"...so you're single, are you, Sarah?" I said, nonchalantly.

Silence again. Jasper gave Conran a malicious swipe across the nose.

Maybe that wasn't such a sensitive thing to say. But, come on, she's not the one who died, you've got to move on at some point.

When she spoke again, she made her voice pierce right into my brain, like a really bad hangover.

"Have you ever lost someone you really loved?"

"No, I..." My English Lit teacher had told me I was like Emma in this regard. Some rubbish about nothing to vex me.

"Well, let me tell you, you don't think about being single, and going out on the scene, and sleeping around – you're too busy trying to hold it all together from one day to the next. Now, look, I need a cheap place to stay, when can I come and look at it." Not a request, an instruction. *God,* she was an old-school butch. Where have you been all my life, Sarah?

"Tomorrow morning" I said to the boys. If she's early enough, I'll let her in, show her the room. But I've got to go back to work – the sick pay's run out. And I can't be late again."

"You think she'll be alright?" Pip looked punch-drunk from the pageant of mad tenants we've had just recently.

"Oh, you know, fine." I breezed. "A bit older than us, I think."

"Let's hope she's better than that little vegan girl." This from Colin, his boyfriend, who was flicking through *Heat*. He was scanning the outfits on the celebs with a critical eye: glancing over each body, discarding, and moving on. Colin is a great dresser himself. He has a proper square jaw and a shaved head, and should be really good looking.

Pip was running around like a manic pixie, tidying up. Well, a pixie on steroids. Pip kind of looks like a stereotypical French chef, if you can imagine that. Tall and broad, soft belly, stubble, but where you'd expect him to have a booming voice, he's hesitant, and obliging. He's not a French chef, he's actually Irish and doesn't really work. He's sort of a housewife to the rest of us. He never has any money, so he and Colin share a single room and Pip pays a bit when he can. Sometimes you forget Pip's in the room, which is an achievement for such a big man. He's always tidying up, which is great news for someone like me.

He lit some incense sticks, on either side of the massive china Buddha on the TV, then suddenly he was back with the hoover, and started darting in and out of our mismatched sofas. He manouvered the hoover carefully around Colin's feet, which didn't even twitch.

My lusting over Sarah's butch voice aside, we really needed someone normal to move in, who was good for the rent, and who would stay. Strictly speaking the crazy room wasn't big enough or safe enough to rent out, but we had to, to get Brian enough rent each month. My job in the call centre doesn't pay a huge amount, so I'm always strapped. We had to find a tenant who's not too picky to rent the crazy room, and they would have to hide from Brian when he comes round. Our doddery landlord might not have noticed the recent circus of tenant freaks, but he would soon notice the enormous hole in his finances if we didn't come up with some more rent, and quickly.

But we can't take just anyone. Our little household community is surprisingly sensitive. Each of us needs some certainty, even a bit of *kindness*, for our difference reasons. Maybe I need this place to work more than anyone. It's the only home I've known since I got kicked out of my parents', nearly three years ago now. I doubt whether anyone misses me. Skinny, scrawny, dykey, Lydia.

By the way, are you gay? Pretty much everyone in this story is gay, but if you're gay, you'd know that. If you're straight – hello there, and welcome.

I finally got Pip to sit down, but he was still sorting through the junk drawer from the kitchen. I mean he had pulled the whole thing out and had brought it to the lounge so he could sort all the old screws and chopsticks and biros while watching TV with me and Colin. His nimble fingers sorted through, removing grime, testing then rejecting a pen here and there, carefully organising the screws into little bags by size.

Pip's efforts made me feel quite exhausted, as I lounged on the smaller of the two sofas. Colin had some rubbish property programme on the TV, but I knew better than to complain, and I couldn't be bothered to read or anything. A trained gibbon could do my job in the call centre, but it still leaves me really drained, so in my off-time, I don't attempt anything more demanding than getting drunk.

Pip tapped me on the shoulder to give me a present from his junk drawer. "Here, Lydia. Instant lesbian kit. Convert any girl." He handed me an old necklace he'd rescued, onto which he'd threaded a bottle opener, and a mini nail clipper.

"Thanks, Pip." I slung it round my neck. Colin shushed us violently. We fell silent. Then, remembering I had work in the morning, I uncapped a new bottle of vodka, and set about getting wasted. I was feeling sick enough anyway, just going over and over in my head: *we're so behind with the rent.*

It hadn't helped that I'd phoned my mum that day, just to test the waters. I was considering asking her for a bit of money, but she just sounded so cold, so pleased I'd moved out, I steeled myself and made it just a social call. I heard all about my perfect sister and her husband, though. Even though my parents threw me out, I still end up trying to make them happy, and keep the details of my life from them. It's pretty depressing.

Colin sent Pip off into the kitchen to do the washing up. He's pretty bossy but he is a useful person to have in a house. He thinks about things I don't, like having a washing-up rota. He earns more than me, but he has to give most of it to his mum so it all gets cancelled out.

If he hadn't have been in a mood that night, I would have asked him if he thought his other half was OK. Pip's been looking very strained, lately.

We're *so* behind with the rent. I hate that quicksand feeling of getting deeper and deeper into debt. None of us have got anyone to turn to for financial help, all having burnt bridges in one way or another.

Please God, let her stay.

~End Sample Chapter of OUT~
For more go to www.Shadoepublishing.com to purchase
the complete book or for many other delightful offerings.

~ Because a publisher should stand behind their authors~

What do you do when you meet someone who changes everything you know about love and passion?

Paige Harlow is a good girl. She's always known where she was going in life: top grades, an ivy league school, a medical degree, regular church attendance, and a happy marriage to a man. So falling in love with her gorgeous roommate and best friend Alyssa Torres is no small crisis. Alyssa is chasing demons of her own, a medical condition that makes her an outcast and a family dysfunctional to the point of disintegration make her a questionable choice for any stable relationship. But Paige's heart is no longer her own. She must now battle the prejudices of her family, friends, and church and come to peace with her new sexuality before she can hope to win the affections of the woman of her dreams. But will love be enough?

www.shadoepublishing.com

~ Because a publisher should stand behind their authors~

Coming out is hard. Coming out in the public eye is even harder. People think they own a piece of you, your work, and your life, they feel they have the right to judge you. You lose not only friends but fans and ultimately, possibly, your career...or your life.

Cassie Summers is a Southern Rock Star; she came out so that she could feel true to herself. Her family including her band and those important to her support her but there are others that feel she betrayed them, they have revenge on their minds...

Karin Myers is a Rock Star in her own right; she is one of those new super promoters: Manager, go-to gal, agent, public relations expert, and hand-holder all in one. Her name is synonymous with getting someone recognized, promoted, and making money. She only handles particular clients though; she's choosy...for some very specific reasons.

Meeting Cassie at a party there is a definite attraction. She does not however wish to represent her despite her excellent reputation. She fights it tooth and nail until she is contractually required to do so. In nearly costs them more than either of them anticipated....their lives.

~ Because a publisher should stand behind their authors~

As I watch the wormhole start to close, I make one last desperate plea ...
"Please? Please don't make me do this?" I whisper.
"You're almost out of time, Lily. Please, just let go?"
I look down at the control panel. I know what I have to do.

Lilith Madison is captain of the Phoenix, a spaceship filled with an elite crew and travelling through the Delta Gamma Quadrant. Their mission is mankind's last hope for survival.

But there is a killer on board. One who kills without leaving a trace and seems intent on making sure their mission fails. With the ship falling apart and her crew being ruthlessly picked off one by one, Lilith must choose who to trust while tracking down the killer before it's too late.

"A suspenseful...exciting...thrilling whodunit adventure in space...discover the shocking truth about what's really happening on the Phoenix" (Clarion)

www.shadoepublishing.com

~ *Because a publisher should stand behind their authors*~

When Delaney Delacroix is called to locate a missing girl, she never plans on getting caught up with a human trafficking investigation or with the local witch. Meeting with Raelin Montrose changes her life in so many ways that Delaney isn't sure that this isn't destiny.

Raelin Montrose is a practicing Wiccan, and when the ley lines that run under her home tell her that someone is coming, she can't imagine that she was going to solve a mystery and find the love of her life at the same time.

~ Because a publisher should stand behind their authors~

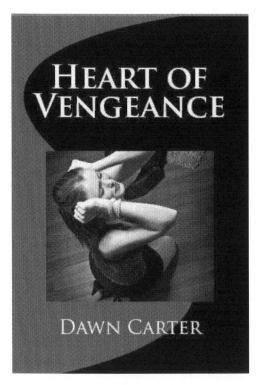

WARNING ~ book contains graphic violence towards women

A serial killer plagues the gay community and leaves a trail of dead bodies across state lines. Agent Danni Pacelli and Agent Parker Stevens rush against time to catch their killer and stop the body count from increasing.

Agent Parker Stevens life was perfect when transferred to a new city and new location which offered her solitude from the grief of losing her partner and children to a predator. But, while hunting down her suspect, she meets Samantha Petrino who takes the once closed off Stevens and opens a world to new love. The charming advertising agent breaks down her defenses, and no matter how hard she fights to protect her heart, she finds herself falling for the beautiful and intelligent woman.

New to the FBI, Agent Danni Pacelli's struggles to balance her personal life along with the job, to save her relationship, she convinces her new partner to bring in Annabel and utilize the young detective's skills to track down their killer or risk losing Annabel all together.

The heroic efforts of two agents who hunt down a serial killer, but find more than they bargained for.

Carrie flees from the demons of her present, trying to protect the ones she loves.

Frankie hides from the demons of her past, and the memory of loved ones she failed to protect.

A modern day princess thrown to the wolves, Carrie's only hope is the rancher who had spent the better part of a decade in self imposed, near total, isolation. Frankie's history of losing those she tries to save haunts her, but this madman threatens her home, her livestock, her sanctuary. She knows she can't do it alone, has she still got enough support from her oldest friends?

~ Because a publisher should stand behind their authors~

KADEN SHAY

New Beginnings

HER CALLING

In a world on the verge of being told that everything they once thought was merely myth is real, can one teenage girl cope with life changes she never saw coming?

Seventeen year old Kyndle Callahan began her year as a typical high school senior. Well, as typical as a girl can be while living life as a werewolf. She wasn't bitten or scratched as most people believe all werewolves are made, no, she was born into the pack that's always been her extended family. She's never seen the people she grew up with as the monsters of myth and legend but everything in her life is thrown into a tailspin when her father springs some shocking news on her. Suddenly, reality as a werewolf is much scarier than the stories humans tell. Stunned by the prospect of spending her life bonded to someone she can't even stand sharing the same space with and devastated at the thought of losing the only love she's ever known, can Kyndle settle into who and what she is in time to set things right? Can the girl that grew up knowing only pack law stand up, embrace her true calling, and become the woman she was meant to be despite going against everything her family believes?

With the help of her best friend Abbey, Kyndle must navigate a confusing world of wolf culture, teenage drama, and coming out in a group that believes her lifestyle is unnatural. Follow her journey through pain, heartache, several states, and the fight to be with the girl she loves and take her place in the world.

~ Because a publisher should stand behind their authors~

Roberta Pena finally has her dream job of being a Biology Teacher at the high school that she once attended, but something sinister lurks in her classroom. She begins to have unusual paranormal experiences. Is she simply losing her mind or is there a ghost trying to make contact? How will she deal with the mystery of the room that often smells of death and where she has begun to have so many unsettling and ghastly sightings? Will she solve the mystery or be forced to leave her career that she worked so hard to achieve? Might she find love in the process?

www.shadoepublishing.com

If you have enjoyed this book and the others listed here Shadoe Publishing is always looking for first, second, or third time authors. Please check out our website @ www.shadoepublishing.com For information or to contact us @ shadoepublishing@gmail.com.

We may be able to help you make your dreams of becoming a published author come true.